SPECIAL DELIVERY

"Teenager Magazine," Ellen read over Jessica's shoulder. "Did you order something from Teenager Magazine?"

"No," Jessica said, "not that I remember." Suddenly, she did remember. She'd entered that contest!

Jessica's stomach suddenly felt queasy. "I think I'll open this later."

"Don't be silly, Jessica," Janet said. "It came special delivery. That means it's important. You have to open it right away."

So, with everybody standing around looking at her, Jessica opened the envelope.

"Congratulations, Mademoiselle Wakefield," Jessica read out loud, in an unsteady voice. "You and your outstanding French-oriented family have been selected as finalists in our Model Family contest. You are eligible to win a week-long trip to Paris. One of our local representatives will contact you in the next few days to set up a visit with you and your family. Good luck!"

For a few seconds, there was silence. Then Mary said, in an awestruck voice, "A week in Paris! Wow, Jessica, that's fantastic! How lucky can you get?"

Bantam Skylark Books in the SWEET VALLEY TWINS series
Ask your bookseller for the books you have missed

SWEET VALLEY TWINS

Mademoiselle
Jessica

◇

NEW

RL 4, 008–012

MADEMOISELLE JESSICA
A Bantam Skylark Book / March 1991

*Sweet Valley High® and Sweet Valley Twins are trademarks of
Francine Pascal*

Conceived by Francine Pascal

*Produced by Daniel Weiss Associates, Inc.
33 West 17th Street
New York, NY 10011*

ISBN 0-553-15849-X

Published simultaneously in the United States and Canada

---

*Bantam Books are published by Bantam Books, a division of Bantam
Doubleday Dell Publishing Group, Inc. Its trademark, consisting of
the words "Bantam Books" and the portrayal of a rooster, is Registered
in U.S. Patent and Trademark Office and in other countries. Marca
Registrada. Bantam Books, 666 Fifth Avenue, New York, New York
10103.*

PRINTED IN THE UNITED STATES OF AMERICA

OPM   0 9 8 7 6 5 4 3 2 1

112216

One

◇

"What do you think, Elizabeth?" Amy Sutton asked, pointing proudly at her new red bike, which was parked in front of Sweet Valley Middle School. "Isn't it the greatest? My parents got it for me to replace the one that burned up in the fire."

Elizabeth Wakefield grinned at Amy. "Looks like the perfect bike for a Friday afternoon ride." She turned to her twin sister, Jessica. "How about it, Jess? Amy and Brooke and I are going for a ride along the beach. Want to come along?"

Jessica Wakefield shook her head. "Brooke isn't going with you, Elizabeth. She's coming to the Dairi Burger with me and the Unicorns."

At that moment, Brooke Dennis, a tall, pretty girl with wavy brown hair and big brown eyes, came up to join them. Brooke had moved to Sweet Valley only a few months before, but she had already made lots of friends.

"Hey, that's a *great* bike, Amy," Brooke said enthusiastically. "All ready for our ride?"

"But Lila said you were coming to the Dairi Burger," Jessica said, sounding surprised. "She told me to meet you after school and walk with you."

Brooke raised her eyebrows. "Lila did mention something about getting together at the Dairi Burger, but I told her I was busy this afternoon. I'm sorry, Jessica. Please tell her I'll come some other time."

Jessica looked disappointed, but she just nodded. "Sure. See you guys later," she called over her shoulder as she left.

"I hope I didn't make Jessica mad," Brooke said. "I didn't know Lila was counting on me to be there."

"I'm sure Jessica understands," Elizabeth reassured her. Elizabeth usually had a pretty good idea of what Jessica was thinking. The two sisters were identical twins. With their long, sun-streaked blond hair, sparkling blue-green eyes, and the tiny dimples that appeared when they smiled, it was hard to tell them apart. But Elizabeth, who was four minutes older, often thought of herself as Jessica's "big sister." Most of the time, Elizabeth did act more grown up. She was serious about her schoolwork and about reading. She particularly enjoyed working with her friends on the newspaper she had helped to start, the *Sweet Valley Sixers*. And, above all else, Elizabeth was a true friend.

Jessica, on the other hand, couldn't be bothered with anything that took as much planning and work as a school paper. She was a member of the Unicorn Club, a group of the prettiest and most popular girls at school. Elizabeth didn't like the club much and had nicknamed it the Snob Squad. Jessica was also a member of the Boosters, the sixth-grade cheerleading squad. When she wasn't going to Unicorn meetings or practicing cheers with the Boosters, she was on the phone with her friends, talking about boys and the latest fashions.

Despite Elizabeth's comment, Brooke looked a little concerned. "I hope you're right about Jessica," she said. She turned to Elizabeth. "Can we go to my house first? I want to change into something cooler."

"Sure thing," Elizabeth said happily. The three of them started for Brooke's house.

"Hi, Jessica," Mary Wallace said, as Jessica brought her soda over to the booth where a group of Unicorns was sitting. Each of the girls was wearing something purple, the color of royalty. The Unicorns tried to wear something purple every day.

Jessica slid into the seat next to Mary. "Hi, Mary," she said. "Hi, everybody."

Across the table, Lila Fowler held out her arm. She was wearing a new charm bracelet. "I was just showing everyone the new bracelet my father bought for me," she said smugly.

Lila was very pretty, with shoulder-length, light brown hair. She lived with her father, one of Sweet Valley's wealthier men. Mr. Fowler gave Lila almost anything she asked for, and lately she'd had plenty to talk about. Lila had just finished having her room redecorated just the way she wanted it, which included new furniture, and she and her father had recently gone to Los Angeles so she could buy an expensive new stereo. But the most exciting thing her father had done was to fly the two of them to Hawaii for a long weekend. Whenever Lila mentioned the Hawaiian trip, Jessica felt very envious, and Lila made sure she had plenty of opportunities to talk about it. Jessica had never taken a trip further than San Diego, and she had had to go on the bus for that one.

This afternoon Jessica was determined not to show Lila how jealous she felt. She glanced at Lila's bracelet and said "Very pretty, Lila," in a casual, offhand way.

"Where's Brooke?" Lila asked, resting her arm on the table so that everybody would have to look at her bracelet. "I thought she was coming with you."

"Brooke had other plans," Jessica said, shoving her straw into her drink. "She said she'd already told you she couldn't come."

Lila frowned. "She did mention something about—" She broke off. "It doesn't matter. In fact, it's probably better that she had something else to do. It gives us a chance to talk about her."

"Talk about her?" Kimberly Haver asked curiously. "Why?"

Lila didn't answer right away. She turned her bracelet so that it caught the light. "I have an idea," she said, lowering her voice so that nobody at the next table could hear her. "Janet has been saying that we need some new people in the club." Janet Howell was the president of the Unicorns, and Lila's cousin.

"How about Mandy Miller?" Ellen suggested.

Lila looked shocked. "Mandy the Clown? Are you serious?"

Ellen giggled. "Of course not. But she's been hanging around us for weeks. And she

6 SWEET VALLEY TWINS

hinted to Caroline Pearce that she wanted to join."

Jessica made a face. Mandy Miller was a little strange. Her clothes looked as if they came from a secondhand store. But Jessica had to admit that Mandy was very funny, and she'd do anything for anybody, especially for Jessica.

"Mandy Miller is *not* Unicorn material," Lila declared. "I was thinking of asking Brooke Dennis."

"Brooke?" Mary asked, sounding surprised.

"Of course," Lila replied. She began to tick off reasons on her fingers. "She's pretty, she's sophisticated, she wears great clothes—"

"Her father is famous," Kimberly put in. Brooke's father was a Hollywood screenwriter. "He knows everybody in the movie business. And Brooke spent one summer in Paris with her mom," she added.

"Well, I'll bet Paris isn't as exciting as Honolulu." Lila reached for her purse. "As a matter of fact, I just happen to have some pictures . . ."

"She throws terrific parties, too," Jessica said quickly. A few weeks before, Brooke and her father had given a huge party at their new house. Jessica's mother had redecorated it for them, so the entire Wakefield family had been invited to the party. Mr. Dennis had also invited the cast of his latest movie, *Car Capers*, as well as the hot new rock group Dynamo. Brooke had asked the Unicorns to help her with some decorations for the party and everybody who had been there was still raving about what a terrific time they had had.

"Inviting her to be a member is a great idea," Kimberly said. "Why didn't we think of it before?"

Lila looked pleased. "We didn't think of it before because we didn't really know Brooke before," she said. "But since the party, I've seen a lot of her. Brooke offered to help me pick out my stereo. Her father knows some people who have a shop in Los Angeles, so she went there with me and my father. You all remember, don't you, that my father just bought me a fantastic new stereo?"

Jessica sighed. She hated it when Lila started bragging about her latest possessions.

"She went shopping with me, too," Ellen said. "She has great taste when it comes to clothes. You know, her father used to hire a fashion consultant to buy her clothes. But she shops for herself now, and she still looks as if she stepped out of an ad in *Image* magazine."

"You see?" Lila said triumphantly. "Looks, clothes, personality. Brooke has absolutely everything it takes to be a Unicorn."

Mary looked thoughtful. "But do you think

she wants to be a Unicorn?" she asked. "She had a chance to try out for the Boosters, remember? She decided not to because she wanted to work on the *Sixers*. If she thought the school newspaper was more important than the Boosters, she probably wouldn't be interested in the Unicorns."

"That's ridiculous," Lila said scornfully. "Nobody would turn down a chance to be a Unicorn."

"Elizabeth did," Kimberly remarked, with a glance at Jessica.

Jessica squirmed uncomfortably, wishing that Kimberly hadn't brought up the subject. In the beginning of the year, Elizabeth had rejected the Unicorns' offer of membership. Jessica would never understand why her twin hadn't wanted to join.

"Yes, but that's *Elizabeth*," Lila said crossly. "We knew she wasn't right for the Unicorns. We only asked her because of Jessica. Anyway, nobody but Elizabeth would turn us down. It's such an incredible honor to be invited."

"It might be embarrassing for us if Brooke did turn us down," Mary said cautiously. "I mean, if word got around that we had asked her and she had said no."

"She's not going to say no," Lila replied firmly. "I'm a hundred-percent positive that Brooke is dying to be a Unicorn."

Mary nodded. "Still, it might be a good idea to see what she thinks first."

"I'll call her tomorrow," Lila said. "And then I'll talk it over with Janet. If Janet likes the idea, we can call a special meeting to discuss Brooke's membership."

"That's good," Ellen said. "Let us know what Brooke says."

Lila reached for her purse again and pulled out a package of photographs. "As I was saying, I have a few pictures of Honolulu. Wait until you see the condo where my father and I stayed." She rolled her eyes dramatically. "It had the most *fabulous* pool, with a waterfall and flowers all around. It even had a sauna. And my father told room service to let me order anything I wanted." She fanned out the pictures on the table so that everybody could see them.

Jessica frowned. She didn't want to hear Lila go on and on about her wonderful father and all the terrific things he did for her. But she could never let Lila know how she felt. Jessica's jealousy would only spur Lila to brag more.

When everybody had admired the photos, Lila tucked them back in her purse. "I bought a few souvenirs, too," she said casually. "The next time you're all at my house, I'll show them to you."

"You are so lucky, Lila," Ellen said with an

envious sigh. "I wish I had a father who would take me to Hawaii."

Lila looked around the table to gather her friends' attention. "But there's more," she said with a superior smile. "I haven't told you the best part yet!"

"The best part?" Kimberly asked. "You mean, there's something better than going to Hawaii for the weekend?"

Lila laughed. "Yes! Jessica, remember when I told you my Dad had a big surprise for me that would make everybody, including Brooke, just green with envy?"

Jessica thought for a moment and tried to remember. She recalled Lila mentioning a special surprise the day Sweet Valley Middle School had gone to the aquarium after the oil spill.

"Yes, I remember," Jessica replied with a shrug.

Lila continued, "You've heard that Dynamo is coming back to Sweet Valley to give a concert?" Dynamo had played several numbers at the Dennises' party, and everybody was anxious to hear more.

"Have we *heard*?" Ellen replied. "Everybody's talking about it." She sighed. "I just adore Nick England. He's so cute."

Lila smiled smugly. "*I* get to watch Dynamo from a sky box at the Arena," she said triumphantly. "My father leased the whole box."

"A sky box!" Ellen whispered reverently.

Jessica bit her lip. The sky boxes were fancy, enclosed boxes high up in the top of the Arena and were reserved for VIP's. They cost hundreds of dollars to lease. Never in a million years could she talk her father into leasing a sky box!

"The box has closed circuit TV," Lila added. "And if you want something to eat or drink during the concert, all you do is push a little button and somebody comes to take your order."

"Wow," Kimberly breathed.

"That's terrific!" Mary said.

"I'd ask you to come and sit in the box with me," Lila said, trying her best to sound regretful, "but I can't. My father has clients coming in from out of town, so there won't be any extra seats."

Jessica frowned. A seat in the sky box, with closed circuit TV and anything you wanted to eat and drink! Why couldn't *she* have been the only child of a father who spoiled her rotten?

Mary finished the last of her soda. "I have to go now," she said, glancing at her watch. "We're having company for dinner and I have to help."

"I have to go, too." Jessica jumped up, glad for the chance to get away from Lila.

Jessica and Mary said good-bye to everybody. When the two of them were out on the sidewalk, Mary shook her head. "Sometimes I get pretty sick of Lila's stories."

"Me, too," Jessica said forcefully. "I wish I could think of a way to shut her up, once and for all."

Mary laughed. "Are you kidding? Lila Fowler was born to brag, and her father makes sure that she'll never run out of things to brag about. The day she stops will be the end of the world."

"I don't think I can wait that long," Jessica muttered.

Elizabeth was having a terrific afternoon at the beach with Amy and Brooke. The three of them had ridden for what seemed like miles along the clean white sand. Then they had parked their bikes and splashed in the surf until they were tired. Now they were sitting on the sand, enjoying the late afternoon sun.

"What a great afternoon," Elizabeth said happily, sifting sand through her fingers. Only a short time ago, an oil spill had marred the beauty of the Sweet Valley beach and had seriously threatened the lives of the birds, fish, and sea mammals. But with a lot of hard work, the beach had been cleaned up and the lives of many animals had been saved.

"This is *so* much better than sitting in the

Dairi Burger with the Unicorns," Brooke said with a satisfied sigh.

Amy was stretched out on her back. A baseball cap was pulled down over her eyes to shade them. "Anything is better than sitting around with the Unicorns," she said with a short laugh. "I mean, I like to talk about boys, and I even like to go shopping. But there can be too much of a good thing, and that's definitely true with the Unicorns. All they talk about are boys and clothes."

"And about Lila's latest triumph," Brooke said. She shook her head. "Unfortunately, Lila's favorite topic of conversation is Lila."

Amy sat up and pushed back her baseball cap. "Brooke, if you don't like Lila, why have you been spending so much time with her lately?"

For a moment, Brooke didn't answer. When she finally spoke her voice sounded thoughtful. "When I was getting ready for the party, Lila and the Unicorns were a lot of help. They were pretty nice, too, and I began to wonder if I hadn't been wrong about them."

"Wrong about them?" Elizabeth asked.

Brooke shrugged. "I hadn't forgotten the time they asked me to try out for the Boosters. They only wanted me because they knew my father could get them passes to Kent Kellerman's set." Sixteen-year-old Kent Kellerman was a TV star. An episode of his popular show "All the World" had been filmed in Sweet Valley some time before and the Unicorns had been dying to get on the set. After Brooke had gotten passes for them, they had suddenly stopped being friendly to her.

"Yeah," Amy agreed. "They're pretty good at using people. They sure used me, after my house burned down."

Brooke gave Amy a sympathetic glance. "Still," she went on, "I thought I might be wrong. There wasn't any harm in giving them a second chance. Then, after the party, Lila started inviting me to do things." She laughed. "At first, it was even kind of fun. But there's something wrong with Lila's mouth. It never stops going. She'll take something nice, like her weekend in Hawaii, and blow it up into something enormous."

"I guess when you've lived in Paris for a summer, the way you have," Amy teased, "a weekend in Hawaii isn't such a big deal."

Elizabeth frowned a little. "Have you told Lila how you feel?"

"Would she listen, even if I told her?" Brooke countered.

Amy laughed. "You're right, Brooke. Lila wouldn't hear you, even if you shouted."

"I've decided the best thing to do is to kind of back off from the friendship," Brooke said.

"If I keep putting her off and turning down invitations, I'm sure that pretty soon she'll get the idea."

Elizabeth grinned. "And what are you going to do with all the time you won't be spending with Lila?"

Brooke grinned back. "Spend it with you and Amy. For starters, I was wondering if you guys would go shopping with me at the mall tomorrow. You know that my father lets me buy my own clothes now. Tomorrow, I'm going to buy a top I saw in the window at Wilson's."

"That sounds terrific," Amy said enthusiastically. "I still need to get a few things to replace what I lost in the fire."

"And I need some new sneakers," Elizabeth said.

"So we'll go, then," Brooke said happily. "We'll have a great time."

Two

◇

Jessica was already in a bad mood when the phone rang. At her mother's orders, she had spent a whole hour cleaning out her closet. Cleaning was definitely not her favorite way to spend a beautiful Saturday morning.

The phone call made Jessica's bad mood even worse. Lila carried on for ten whole minutes about the terrific sky box seat her father had gotten her for the Dynamo concert. She was already trying to decide which of her new outfits she should wear and which restaurant she should ask her father to take her to before the concert.

"Where do *you* think I should tell him to take me, Jessica?" Lila wanted to know.

Jessica felt like stamping her foot and screaming "Give me a break, Lila!" But she didn't. Instead, she suggested a little sarcastically that they go to Guido's Pizza Palace. "You could throw pennies into their artificial waterfall and wish you were back in Hawaii," Jessica said. *Maybe that wouldn't be such a bad idea*, she told herself. *If Lila were back in Hawaii, I wouldn't have to listen to her!*

"Very funny, Jessica," Lila said acidly. "I have to think of someplace really special. After all, it's going to be one of the biggest nights of my life. Can you imagine? Closed circuit TV! It'll be like having Dynamo right in the box, so close that Nick England could put his arms around me!" She sighed. "Jessica, I have such a fabulous father. He gives me absolutely everything I ask for."

Jessica's frayed patience finally snapped. "I've got to go, Lila," she said. Without waiting for an answer, she banged down the receiver.

"It isn't fair!" she muttered, thinking how much fun it would be if *she* could sit in the sky box and watch Nick England on closed circuit TV.

What was even worse, she realized, was that she didn't have anything to brag to Lila about. Her family was just a regular family.

Jessica threw herself down on her bed and picked up her latest copy of *Teenager Magazine*.

What would it be like to be in Lila's shoes, she wondered enviously, the only child of a wealthy father who loved giving presents? She flipped through the pages of the magazine and looked at the pictures of gorgeous teenage girls wearing high-fashion outfits, posed against exotic backdrops. What would it be like to be one of *those* girls?

She turned a page and her eye caught an attractive ad. The picture showed a teenage girl and her family sitting in a charming French sidewalk cafe. Red-striped umbrellas shaded the small tables and red geraniums cascaded over the sides. Under the picture in big letters was printed, "Win a Fabulous Week in Paris for You and Your Family!"

Jessica's eyes narrowed. There was absolutely no comparison between a fabulous week in Paris and a weekend trip to Hawaii. Quickly, Jessica scanned the paragraphs under the picture. There was something about eligibility and a lot of fine print that she couldn't see without squinting.

What she could read was very interesting. The contest was being sponsored by *Teenager Magazine* and its French counterpart, *Le Teen*. The magazines were searching for the perfect American family and the perfect French family. The first prize for the American family was an all-expense-paid trip to Paris. All you had to do to enter was to write an essay describing your family and telling just how perfect they were. Nothing could be easier, if, of course, you just happened to have a perfect family that was particularly interested in French things. Jessica frowned. Her family was pretty neat, but they weren't particularly French-oriented.

Jessica turned the page to find a preaddressed, postage-paid envelope and an entry blank on which to write the contest essay. She stared at it for a moment and imagined what she would say if she were really going to enter. Then, on an impulse, she tore out the page and reached for a pen. She knew she wasn't actually going to win the trip to Paris because her family wasn't interested in French things. But she could still dream. The entry blank gave her a chance to describe the absolutely perfect family, the family that would put Lila to shame.

For the next hour, Jessica let her imagination run wild. First, she described her mother, a beautiful blonde who worked part-time as an interior decorator and who spent the rest of her time cooking gourmet food. French, of course. Jessica frowned. There ought to be something else she could say about her mother. After all, most of what she had already written was true. Then she had an idea. Her mother was also very interested in the ballet, she wrote. *That's true*, Jessica thought. It was her mother's idea that she and Elizabeth take ballet lessons at the Dance Studio, and she came to watch whenever Madame Andre's class gave a recital. It took only a little stretch of the imagination to write that her mother was a *prima ballerina* with the Sweet Valley Civic Ballet.

Next, her father. Jessica nibbled on her pen and stared dreamily out the window, trying to imagine the absolutely perfect father. In a few minutes, she had it. Her father, she wrote, was a high-powered lawyer. This was true. But, she added, he was also a well-known artist who showed his oil paintings, of French subjects, of course, in all the local galleries. Jessica had to admit she was stretching this part quite a bit. Her father had a garage workshop where he liked to repaint furniture and do occasional carpentry. He had done a terrific job repainting the end table in the den. In addition to his painting, Jessica continued, he was a terrific father, very generous and helpful, always ready to buy his children what they wanted and to take them on exciting trips. In fact, the family was planning a trip to New York next summer so that her mother could study with a famous French chef, and her father could visit all the art museums. Jessica and Elizabeth planned to shop and see all the Broadway shows. Jessica sighed happily as she read over what she had written.

Next she would describe Steven, her abso-

lutely terrific fourteen-year-old brother. In real
life, of course, Steven was a real pain and
always gave her a hard time. But the fictional
Steven wasn't like that at all. He was always
looking out for his sisters' interests. He was
sweet and brotherly, without being the least bit
patronizing or overprotective. He was also a star
basketball player who won all the games for his
team. That was mostly true, Jessica reflected.
But even more exciting, she added, Steven was
a virtuoso on the trombone. After years of dedi-
cated practice, he had formed his own jazz
ensemble (that was a French word, wasn't it?)
and they were now touring the region giving
concerts. Of course, the real story was very different. Steven had just started taking trombone
lessons a few months before. He couldn't make
much music yet, although he certainly made a
lot of noise. But he was playing third trombone
in Beginner Band, and the family had recently
gone to the high school to hear the band play.
Jessica grinned at what she had written. A
sweet big brother, a star basketball player, and
a trombone virtuoso with his own jazz group.
A brother like that would really be someone to
brag about!

Now it was Elizabeth's turn. Jessica looked
at the page. She couldn't think of a way to make
Elizabeth any more perfect than she already
was, so she wrote mostly the truth. Elizabeth

was extremely pretty. She was an excellent student who made straight As and who still had time to start up a class newspaper—with a column written in French. She was a loyal sister who always stood up for her twin. She was a terrific friend who was never too busy to stop what she was doing and lend a hand. Not only that . . . Jessica made herself stop. If she wrote any more wonderful things about Elizabeth, even if most of them were true, no one would believe them!

The only person left to write about was herself. How should she describe herself, as a member of this absolutely fantastic family? Well, for one thing, Jessica wrote, she was a great student, just as good as her twin, Elizabeth. In addition, she was a member of the Boosters, the sixth-grade cheerleading squad. She was also a member of the Unicorns, an exclusive girls' club that. . . . Jessica frowned. What should she write about the Unicorns? Actually, they didn't do all that much, except hold meetings, go shopping, and give parties. Jessica knew that sounded pretty self-centered. So instead, she wrote that the Unicorns were a service group that took on different kinds of community projects. Recently they had done volunteer work in the local hospital and at the local library.

Of course, Jessica added as an afterthought, she spoke French quite well. As a matter of fact, the entire family spoke *only* French at home. It made the dinner-table conversation much more interesting. And both she and Elizabeth, she went on, loved doing crossword puzzles, naturally, in French.

Jessica sat back and stared dreamily out the window. What an incredibly terrific family the Wakefields were! With a family like that, she was sure to win the contest. And if she won the contest, Lila would have to shut up about her father.

Jessica looked back down at her essay. It needed just one final touch. She would write *au revoir* at the bottom and sign her name.

But when she started to write the French phrase, she realized that she didn't know how to spell it. There was a French dictionary on her father's desk downstairs. With her essay in her hand, Jessica went downstairs to check the dictionary. Carefully, she copied the spelling and signed her name with a flourish. Then she smelled the enticing aroma of fresh chocolate-chip cookies, so she picked up her essay and took it into the kitchen.

"Help yourself to cookies," Mrs. Wakefield said, looking up from her work which was spread across the kitchen table.

Jessica took one and glanced at the plans on the table. "Do you have a new project?"

Mrs. Wakefield's blue eyes twinkled. "Yes.

Brooke Dennis's father helped me get it. And you'll never guess who—"

Just then the telephone rang. Jessica put down her essay and her half-eaten cookie to answer it.

"Hi, Jessica," Lila said.

"Hi, Lila." Jessica felt much friendlier than she'd felt just an hour ago. Writing about her perfect family had done her a lot of good.

"I've just talked to Brooke on the phone," Lila announced.

"Good," Jessica said. "Did you ask her whether or not she wants to be a Unicorn?"

"I didn't think it was a good idea to come straight out and ask," Lila said. "So I hinted around. I told her how terrific the Unicorns are, and I said it was time that we added another member to the club."

"What did she say?" Jessica asked, eying the other chocolate-chip cookies.

"She said the Unicorns sounded like a lot of fun, and she was glad the club was expanding a little."

Jessica frowned. "Is that all she said? That doesn't sound very enthusiastic to me."

"Well, what did you expect?" Lila demanded. "Did you think she'd jump up and down and wave both arms and yell, 'I want to be a Unicorn'? There's a certain way these things are done, Jessica. Brooke is playing it very cool, and that's good. After all, we wouldn't want her if she were too eager, would we?"

"I guess not," Jessica said. She thought that Brooke could have shown a little more enthusiasm, but Lila was probably right. There was a certain etiquette to being invited into an exclusive club.

"I was wondering if you'd like to come to the mall with me this afternoon," Lila said.

"That sounds great!" Jessica exclaimed, forgetting all about how upset she had been with Lila. She turned to her mother. "Mom, is it OK if I go to the mall with Lila?"

Mrs. Wakefield nodded. "Of course. Have a good time, honey."

"I'm on my way," Jessica told Lila. She hung up the phone, grabbed two more cookies, and dashed to the closet to get her jacket. "See you, Mom," she called. Then she ran out the door, leaving her contest entry on the kitchen counter beside the phone.

"Hi, Mom," Elizabeth said, coming into the kitchen a few minutes later. Amy and Brooke were behind her. She glanced at the drawings on the kitchen table. "Do you have a new project?"

"Yes, and it's really interesting," Mrs. Wakefield said. She smiled at Brooke. "Your father helped me get it, Brooke."

Brooke looked down at the drawings. "Is this the house that Nick England is buying for his parents?"

Mrs. Wakefield nodded. "It's going to be a real challenge, too."

"Nick England?" Amy asked excitedly. "The singer from Dynamo?"

"That's the one," Mrs. Wakefield said with a laugh. She pointed to the cookies on the counter. "Help yourself to cookies, girls."

"Thanks," Elizabeth said happily. "I'm going to get my Scrabble set, and then we're going over to Amy's house."

"Fine," Mrs. Wakefield said absently, looking down at her drawings again.

The girls took several cookies and headed upstairs.

"Don't you think that Lila was sounding you out about being a Unicorn?" Elizabeth asked Brooke.

Brooke shook her head. "No, I'm sure that's not what she had on her mind. After I turned down the Boosters, why would she think I'd want to be a Unicorn? But it did seem as if she thought I'd be interested in them. She went on about how great it was to be a Unicorn, telling me how you got to go to all these interesting meetings and fabulous parties."

"Yeah, really interesting meetings," Amy

put in sarcastically. "Where they sit around and gossip about who's going out with who."

Brooke nodded. "And then she said that the club wasn't quite as big as they wanted it to be and that there was going to be a vacancy pretty soon."

Elizabeth glanced at Brooke. "What did you say?"

"What could I say?" Brooke answered with a shrug. "I told her it was nice that the club was expanding. And if you ask me, it would be a good thing if they did get bigger. The Unicorns are too exclusive." She laughed. "They ought to invite a few dozen new people to be members. But not me!"

Amy gave Brooke a look of mock horror. "You mean, you're not absolutely *dying* to be a Unicorn? Just think of all the things you'll miss out on, like finding out who Bruce Patman kissed at the last dance, or trying to decide which purple blouse to wear with your purple skirt and your purple sneakers."

Brooke made a face. "I'd look like a grape in all that purple. And I don't like Bruce Patman."

Elizabeth got her Scrabble set out of the closet. "If you don't become a Unicorn," she said as the girls headed downstairs, "you'll also miss out on doing a pledge task. Actually," she added, "I don't think you'll miss much. The pledge is usually asked to play a dirty trick on somebody, and nobody thinks it's very funny except for the Unicorns."

"Elizabeth," Mrs. Wakefield said, as the girls walked through the kitchen, "I've written a letter to Grandma. It's there on the counter, next to the phone. Would you drop it into the corner box on your way to Amy's?"

"Sure, Mom," Elizabeth said. She went over to the counter and picked up the envelope. Then she spotted Jessica's contest entry form. "There's something here that's got Jessica's name on it," she said. "But it's not folded or sealed. Do you think she wants it mailed?"

"I imagine she does," Mrs. Wakefield answered. "She was talking on the phone to Lila, and she probably just forgot to fold it up."

Elizabeth folded the entry form so that the address was on the outside. Five minutes later, she dropped it into the corner mailbox, along with her mother's letter.

Jessica was sitting on her bed in her pajamas late that evening, flipping through *Teenager Magazine*, when she came to the torn page where the contest entry form had been. She remembered that she had left the entry form on the kitchen counter. She got up and rushed anxiously downstairs. It would be very embarrassing if somebody found it and read what she'd written about the perfect Wakefield family. Steven, especially, would never let her hear the end of it.

But when Jessica got to the kitchen, the counter was bare. She stared at it for a minute, feeling more and more anxious. She had never intended to mail the essay! She went to find her mother, who was watching television in the den.

"I thought you'd already gone to bed, honey," Mrs. Wakefield said.

"I was reading a magazine," Jessica said, "and then I thought of something. Uh, Mom, did you find a . . . something I left on the kitchen counter this afternoon?"

Mrs. Wakefield frowned. "Elizabeth found an envelope. I think she mailed it."

Jessica gulped. *Elizabeth mailed it?* She turned and dashed back upstairs. Elizabeth was in the bathroom, brushing her teeth.

"Lizzie," Jessica cried frantically, "you didn't mail that envelope I left on the kitchen counter this afternoon, did you?"

Elizabeth rinsed out her mouth and turned around. "Yes, I did," she said. "It looked like something important so I dropped it in the mail box on my way to Amy's." She looked closely at Jessica. "What's wrong, Jess? Wasn't it supposed to be mailed?"

Wordlessly, Jessica shook her head. For better or worse, her fabulous fictional family was now officially entered in the contest.

Three

◇

For the next few days, Jessica worried about the contest. Anybody reading her entry form would know in an instant that the Wakefield family was just too good to be true. *No* family could be that perfect. What would the contest officials do when they read her essay? Was there a penalty for writing lies on an official entry form? Would she have to go to jail?

The more days that passed, the more comfortable Jessica began to feel. After all, lots of kids read *Teenager Magazine*. Probably hundreds or even thousands of people had entered the contest. The chances that her entry would be noticed were probably very small. By Thursday, the contest had slipped to the back of Jessica's mind, and by Friday, she had completely forgotten about it.

By the end of the week, Jessica's irritation with Lila was foremost on her mind. She had no time to worry about lost contest entries. Instead, she concentrated on how to stop her friend's bragging once and for all. Jessica wasn't the only one who was annoyed. Several Unicorns complained to one another that they were sick of hearing Lila's stories. Even Ellen was getting tired of it.

But Lila just kept on talking. On Wednesday, she told everybody that her father had just bought her a cordless telephone so that she could talk on the phone while she was sunbathing beside the pool. And on Thursday at lunch, she told them that her father had decided to install a sauna, just like the one at the condo where they'd stayed in Hawaii.

"It will have automatic temperature control and lots of steam," Lila boasted.

"Hot air, she means," Tamara Chase whispered to Jessica. "The same stuff that she's full of."

"I suppose you can take your portable phone into the sauna and talk to us from there," Kimberly Haver remarked with a touch of sarcasm.

But Lila didn't notice Kimberly's tone.

"What a good idea!" she exclaimed. "That's exactly what I'll do!"

Ellen smothered a giggle. "Maybe you can get your father to install closed circuit TV," she said. "That way, you could watch Dynamo while you steam. Or maybe you could invite Nick England to come and steam with you."

Everybody laughed, including Jessica. But she was really getting fed up with Lila. Day after day, she had to listen to the latest thing that Lila's father had bought her or the latest place he had taken her.

But Friday morning in homeroom, Lila held off on her favorite topic of conversation. She told Jessica and Ellen that she had finally talked to Janet about asking Brooke to be a Unicorn.

"What did she say?" Jessica asked eagerly. "Does she think it's a good idea?"

Lila fluffed her brown hair. "Janet agreed with me that Brooke has all the special Unicorn qualities," she said importantly. "She says Brooke would definitely keep up the Unicorn image."

"What does Janet think we ought to do?" Ellen wanted to know.

Lila leaned forward and lowered her voice. "Janet's calling a special, top secret meeting this afternoon to discuss Brooke. We can't ask her to be a member unless everybody wants to invite her. But Janet says that she doesn't think there'll be any disagreement."

Ellen nodded. "We haven't had a new Unicorn since we made Belinda Layton a member. But Belinda is so busy with sports that she hardly ever comes to meetings."

"That's why it's important to ask somebody who is really committed to being a Unicorn," Jessica remarked. "Belinda's nice, and every time she wins a game she makes us look good. But it would be better if she'd show up for a few meetings."

"Brooke won't miss any meetings," Lila said confidently. "She'll want to be involved in everything we do."

Jessica frowned a little. "Why is this meeting top secret?"

"We don't want Brooke finding out that we want to ask her," Ellen pointed out. "That way, if for some reason the members decide against her, there won't be any bad feelings."

"That won't happen," Lila said with assurance. "Everybody will want Brooke as a Unicorn. But just the same, the meeting is *top secret*. Don't tell anyone." She looked at Jessica. "Not even Elizabeth."

"Of course not," Jessica said.

"Absolutely," Ellen agreed.

"But of course," Caroline Pearce said in a loud whisper, "nobody's supposed to know."

Elizabeth stared at Caroline. The girls were

in the locker room, changing for gym class. "If it's such a secret," she asked, "how did you find out that the Unicorns are going to invite Brooke to be a member?"

"Sshh!" Caroline looked around to make sure that nobody was listening. "I have my sources," she said importantly. "Anyway, I didn't say they were definitely going to invite Brooke. I said they were going to *discuss* her."

"Discuss me?" Brooke asked curiously, coming over to join them. She put one foot up on the bench to tie her gym sneaker. "Who's going to discuss me?"

Caroline looked smug. "The Unicorns," she said, flipping her red hair over her shoulder. "They're having a meeting this afternoon."

Brooke laughed. "What are they discussing *me* for? Did I do something they didn't approve of?"

"They're discussing whether they want to invite you to become a member," Elizabeth said. She watched Brooke to see how she would react to the news.

Brooke raised one eyebrow. "Me? A Unicorn? So that's what Lila was getting at on the phone on Saturday. I knew she must have had a reason for telling me about how great the Unicorns are. But I honestly didn't think they were going to ask me to join." She looked at Elizabeth. "Has Jessica said anything to you?"

Elizabeth shook her head. "Not a word."

"There, you see?" Brooke said. "I'm sure it's just a rumor. If they were going to ask me, Jessica would have told you."

"Not if it's supposed to be a secret." Caroline looked meaningfully at Brooke. "Being a Unicorn is a big honor. Since you're fairly new here, Brooke, maybe you don't understand just what an honor it really is."

"I think I do," Brooke said, laughing a little. "But it's an honor I'm not sure I'm ready to accept. Somehow, I just don't think that the Unicorns are exactly my style."

Caroline's green eyes grew wide. "You mean you don't want to be a Unicorn?" she asked incredulously. "But everybody at Sweet Valley Middle School wants to be a Unicorn! Well, almost everybody." Caroline glanced at Elizabeth.

Brooke grinned and draped her arm over Elizabeth's shoulders. "Actually, Elizabeth and I were thinking of starting a club of our own." She wrinkled up her forehead, pretending to think. "Let's see, what were we going to call ourselves? The Zebras?"

"I thought we were going to be the Rhinos," Elizabeth said, playing along with Brooke's joke. "Since the Unicorns have a horn, we ought to have one too. And rhinos are an endangered species. They're almost as rare as unicorns."

Brooke burst out laughing. "That's good, Elizabeth. We'll call ourselves the Rhinos. Caroline, would you like to be a Rhino?"

Caroline looked from one to the other. "I have a feeling that you guys are making a joke out of this," she said suspiciously.

Elizabeth and Brooke looked at one another and giggled.

Brooke grabbed a volleyball from under the bench and tossed it to Elizabeth. "Come on, let's play ball!"

Out on the floor, Ms. Langberg, the gym teacher, lined everybody up for a volleyball game. Elizabeth, Brooke, and Caroline ended up on the same team. Lila and Ellen were together on the other team. When Ms. Langberg blew her whistle, Caroline served the first ball. Ellen punched it back across the net, straight to Elizabeth. Elizabeth gave it a hard underhand hit and knocked it into the middle of the opposite court. Lila made a halfhearted try for it but missed. The ball rolled across the floor and under the bleachers.

Ms. Langberg blew her whistle and stepped forward. "Move faster next time, Lila," she said. She signaled time out while Nora Mercandy scurried after the ball.

Elizabeth turned to Brooke, who was standing beside her in the back row. "I know that you were joking a few minutes ago," she said quietly. "But how do you *really* feel about joining the Unicorns?"

Brooke pointed across the net. "Hear that?" she asked.

Elizabeth listened. On the other side of the net, Lila was showing off her new charm bracelet to Pamela Jacobson. "Of course it's eighteen-karat gold," she was saying proudly, loud enough so that everybody in the gym could hear. "I wouldn't wear anything else, except sterling silver, of course."

"I don't think I could be a Unicorn," Brooke said. "I couldn't take Lila's chatter for too long."

"Well, what are you going to do if they ask you to join?" Elizabeth asked.

"I guess I'll figure that out when the time comes," Brooke answered. "Anyway, I still don't believe they're really going to ask me."

Caroline caught the ball that Ms. Langberg tossed her and then served it quickly. It sailed cleanly up and over the net.

"It's your ball, Lila," Ellen yelled excitedly. "Get it!"

But Lila was still showing off her bracelet to Pamela and she didn't see the ball. It fell two feet in front of her, bounced up, and smacked her in the face.

"Ow!" Lila exclaimed loudly. Her hand flew to her nose.

"Oops," Caroline said, sounding panicked. "Sorry, Lila. I didn't mean to hit you. I hope you're not hurt."

"My nose is bleeding," Lila said in a muffled voice.

Ms. Langberg looked at her sternly. "You wouldn't have gotten hit if you'd been paying attention to the ball." She took a tissue out of her pocket and handed it to Lila. "Here. Go to the locker room and wash your face."

Jessica sat down next to Ellen in Janet Howell's den. "What's wrong with Lila's nose?" she asked in a low voice. "It looks swollen."

"Caroline Pearce socked her in the face with a volleyball in gym class this morning," Ellen replied. "Lila was showing off her bracelet and didn't even see the ball coming."

"Oh." Jessica knew she ought to feel sorry for Lila, but somehow she couldn't.

Janet Howell stood up and called the meeting to order. "We're here," she announced, "to hold a very important discussion. Lila has proposed that we invite Brooke Dennis into the club. Lila, why don't you tell us why you think Brooke would make a good Unicorn? Then we can talk about her plusses and minuses."

Lila stood up. "I think you all know Brooke,"

she said, looking around at the group. Everybody nodded. "Well," Lila went on, "some of us have been thinking that she's got what it takes to be a Unicorn. She's pretty, she's got a great personality, she wears great clothes, she gives terrific parties, and she's been to lots of places."

Jessica frowned. There was a boastful tone to Lila's voice. Lila sounded as if she were personally taking credit for Brooke's personality and the fabulous things she had done.

"Brooke's father knows everybody there is to know in the movie business," Betsy Gordon put in.

"If you ask me, that's a big plus," Tamara Chase commented. "Having a famous father is really cool."

"Her mother lives in Paris," Kimberly Haver said, "and Brooke speaks French. That's another plus."

"Hey, maybe she could help me with my French," one of the eighth-grade Unicorns said.

"She probably could," Ellen replied. "She speaks it pretty well."

Janet looked around. "OK, that's a lot of plusses. Now, what are her minuses?"

There was silence. Nobody could come up with any minuses.

"No minuses?" Janet asked after a minute. "Come on. Nobody's perfect."

"Brooke is," Lila said triumphantly. "That's

why I'm proposing her for membership. She's the perfect Unicorn."

"Do you get the feeling that she wants to join?" Mary asked.

"Yes, I do," Lila replied. "I talked to her on the phone the other day. She was really enthusiastic. She's dying to join."

Jessica straightened up. That wasn't the way she remembered it. From Lila's report, Brooke hadn't sounded very enthusiastic at all.

"I guess I'm kind of surprised to hear that," Mary said. "I have the feeling that Brooke isn't really sold on the Unicorns. She is working on the *Sixers*, isn't she?"

Everybody turned and looked at Jessica. "Yes, she is," Jessica affirmed. "She helped Elizabeth write that interview with Kent Kellerman."

"But that was weeks ago," Lila pointed out. "Anyway, as far as I'm concerned, Brooke can go on working on the *Sixers* if she wants to. As long as it doesn't interfere with Unicorn business."

Janet looked around. "Let's take a vote. All those in favor of making Brooke a Unicorn say 'aye.'" There was a chorus of ayes. "All those opposed, say 'no.'" Mary looked uncomfortable, but she didn't say anything.

"Terrific," Janet said with satisfaction. "Brooke Dennis will be our next Unicorn."

"I have an idea," Lila said. "I think we should have an afterschool party and invite Brooke to it. At the party, we can surprise her by telling her we want her to join. I'd offer to give the party, now that the patio is finally rebuilt. But my father says that construction on the new sauna is going to start right away, so I can't."

"I'll give the party," Jessica volunteered quickly.

"That's great, Jessica," Janet said. "Let's do it on Monday, OK? The sooner the better."

"What about Brooke's pledge task?" Kimberly wanted to know. "What are we going to ask her to do?"

"I'll appoint a committee to come up with Brooke's pledge task," Janet said. "Jessica, Mary, and Ellen, will you please get together and decide what Brooke ought to do?"

"Great," Jessica replied. She already had some ideas.

"We'll come up with something really cool," Ellen promised. "Something that Brooke won't mind doing at all."

"Then it's settled," Janet said with a tone of finality. "The party will be on Monday, at Jessica's house. Until then, remember, this is all extremely confidential. *Top secret*. We don't want Brooke or anybody else to know until the party. OK?"

Lila turned to Jessica. "That means you can't tell your sister, Jessica. Elizabeth and Brooke are friends, and Elizabeth might spill the beans."

"No, she wouldn't," Jessica protested. "Not if I told her not to. Elizabeth's very good at keeping secrets." *In fact*, Jessica thought, *she's probably better at it than most of the Unicorns.* Betsy Gordon, for example, was always telling the Unicorns' secrets.

"All the same," Janet said firmly, "don't tell Elizabeth. Membership matters are absolutely confidential. We don't share them with *anybody* outside the club." She looked around. "That includes sisters and brothers—and boyfriends."

All the Unicorns agreed. Brooke Dennis's nomination would be top secret until the meeting on Monday. Jessica sighed. She hated to keep secrets from her twin. But she was a Unicorn, and she had to keep her word.

Four

◇

"Hi, Elizabeth."

It was Monday morning, before homeroom, and Elizabeth was getting her books out of her locker when Todd Wilkins stopped to say hello. They had been friends for several years, and good friends since an informal bowling party a few weeks before. Since then, they'd gone bike riding together a couple of times, and they saw one another often at school.

"Hi, Todd," Elizabeth said happily. She was glad that she had worn her favorite blue blouse and taken a little extra care with her hair that morning. She looked around. "Have you seen Brooke and Amy? They're supposed to meet me."

"No, I haven't." Todd said. He brushed his hand through his brown hair. "Hey, what's this I hear about Brooke Dennis?"

"What about Brooke?" Elizabeth asked, taking her English book out of the locker.

"Everybody's saying that she's going to be a Unicorn."

Elizabeth laughed. "That's an old rumor, Todd. Caroline Pearce told me that last week." She paused. "Anyway, if it were true, I'm sure that Jessica would have told me." Jessica didn't always tell her what the Unicorns were doing, but in this case she probably would have because Elizabeth and Brooke were friends.

"Well, it's true, all right," Todd said. "I mean, not that I care a whole lot about the Unicorns. But I heard it from Johnny Gordon, Betsy Gordon's brother."

At that moment, Brooke came up to them. "Hi, Elizabeth. Hi, Todd. Hey, Elizabeth, I heard about the party at your house today."

"A party at my house?" Elizabeth asked, puzzled. "Jessica mentioned having a few Unicorns over after school, but I didn't think it was going to be a party."

"Well, Jessica just invited me," Brooke said. "She said that the Unicorns especially wanted me to come."

"See?" Todd said with an amused twinkle in his brown eyes. "I told you so."

"Told you what?" Brooke looked from Elizabeth to Todd. "What's the big secret?"

"Todd heard a rumor that the Unicorns have decided to ask you to join," Elizabeth replied. She was a little hurt that Jessica hadn't told her. But it really wasn't her business. It was between Brooke and the Unicorns.

"Where did you hear this rumor, Todd?' Brooke demanded.

"From a Unicorn's brother," Todd said with a laugh. "Anyway, it's all over school. I just heard a couple of girls talking about it in the hall. Some of the Unicorns aren't very good at keeping secrets, you know." He laughed again. "You'd better get your purple clothes ready."

Brooke made a face. "Oh, brother."

"Does that mean you don't want to be a Unicorn?" Todd asked teasingly. "Or that you're so overwhelmed with the honor that you're speechless?"

Brooke laughed. "You guess."

Todd grinned. "That's it, Brooke. Keep them wondering." He glanced at his watch. "I've got to go." He gave Elizabeth a warm smile. "See you later, Elizabeth."

Elizabeth said good-bye to Todd and then turned to Brooke. "So what are you going to do?" she asked. "Have you changed your mind? Do you want to join the Unicorns?"

"No, not really." Brooke grinned. "But I

have to admit that I'm beginning to be curious about them. What are the Unicorn meetings like?"

Elizabeth shook her head. "The meeting I went to was so boring it almost put me to sleep. All they did was gossip about clothes and which soap opera star would be the dreamiest dream date. I remember thinking that if I heard 'he's so cute' one more time, I'd get sick."

Brooke laughed. "Come on, Elizabeth, you must be exaggerating. I know that the Unicorns can be pretty silly. But the meeting couldn't have been that bad."

"Well, you've got a chance to see for yourself," Elizabeth said. "You're going to Jessica's party this afternoon, aren't you? It probably won't be much different from a meeting."

"Actually, I hadn't really made up my mind to go," Brooke said. "But after listening to your experience, I think I'll have to go and see for myself."

"Hi, Brooke," Amy called as she hurried toward them. "Hi, Elizabeth. Hey, Brooke, I hear that you're going to be the next Unicorn!"

"Don't count on it," Brooke said. "But Elizabeth's just talked me into going to the meeting this afternoon."

"*Elizabeth* talked you into it?" Amy asked in disbelief.

"I told her about the time I went to a meeting," Elizabeth said with a grin, "and she didn't believe me. So she's decided to see for herself."

Amy laughed. "Well, I hope you have a good time, Brooke. And that you don't die of boredom."

"If I survive," Brooke replied, "maybe we ought to have a meeting of the Rhinos to celebrate. What do you say?"

"We don't have to wait for that," Elizabeth said. "We can do that at lunchtime."

"Great!" Brooke said. She turned away to go to her homeroom. "See you then."

At lunch on Monday, Jessica, Mary, and Ellen got together at the Unicorner, the Unicorns' special table, to come up with a pledge task for Brooke.

Jessica opened her milk carton. "We could have her steal Ms. Langberg's whistle," she suggested.

"Getting her hands on that whistle would be pretty tough," Mary said doubtfully. "I've never seen Ms. Langberg without it. She wears it around her neck as if it were a million-dollar diamond."

"It was pretty tough to swipe Mrs. Arnette's lesson plan book," Jessica retorted, digging into her lasagna. "But I did it. I'll bet Brooke could come up with a way to steal the whistle."

"Yes, but somehow it doesn't seem like the

right pledge task for her." Ellen grinned. "Maybe we ought to ask her to do something really terrible, like stealing Leslie Carlisle's bra."

Jessica giggled. Leslie Carlisle was very developed for her age.

"Hey, you guys, that's too *mean*," Mary said, wrinkling her nose. "If we asked Brooke to do something like that, she'd never go through with it. And I wouldn't blame her, either."

"OK," Ellen said defensively. "I was only kidding."

Jessica leaned forward. "Well, then, how about drawing a cartoon of Mr. Nydick and having Brooke pin it on the map in his room? When he pulls the map down, everybody will see the cartoon and crack up."

"I don't know," Ellen said doubtfully. "That doesn't seem right, either."

"Hi, Jessica," a boy's voice said.

Jessica looked up. "Oh, hi, Aaron," she said in a breezy tone that concealed the excitement she felt. She and Aaron had gotten together at the bowling alley a few weeks before. She had been the first of the sixth-grade Unicorns to have a real boyfriend.

Behind Aaron was Peter Jeffries, Mary's boyfriend, and with them was Rick Hunter, the boy Ellen liked. Peter was carrying a red Frisbee.

"If you guys are done with your lunch," Peter said to the three of them, "how about playing Frisbee with us?"

"There's about fifteen minutes until the next class," Aaron added.

Jessica pushed her tray back. She wasn't quite finished with her lasagna, but she didn't want to miss this chance to be with Aaron. "I'm done," she said. "I'd love to play Frisbee, Aaron."

"But we haven't decided about Brooke's pledge task," Mary reminded her.

"That's OK," Jessica said. "We've got plenty of time. It doesn't have to be done today, does it?"

"Of course not," Ellen said, flashing a special smile at Rick. "Come on, let's go!"

After school, Jessica hurried home to put out the cookies, chips, and soda she'd bought for the party. Ten minutes later, most of the Unicorns had gathered in the Wakefields' den. In another few minutes, Brooke arrived with Lila and Ellen.

"We're so glad you could come this afternoon, Brooke," Janet said. She gave Brooke an approving glance. "I like your outfit. That green top is really cute."

"Thanks," Brooke said. "And thanks for inviting me. I was a little surprised. I didn't think the Unicorns invited nonmembers to their meetings."

"This isn't exactly a meeting," Jessica said, handing Brooke a soda. "It's a combination meeting and party."

"A party for you," Lila added.

Brooke looked at her curiously. "For me?"

"Yes," Lila said. "We asked you to come because—"

"I think *I* should be the one to tell her, Lila," Janet said crossly.

"Well, then, tell her," Lila retorted.

Janet rapped on the coffee table for attention. "Welcome, everybody," she said, in her take-charge voice. "I think you all know that we have a special guest this afternoon. Brooke Dennis hasn't lived in Sweet Valley very long, but she's been here long enough to know that the Unicorns are a very special group of girls, both beautiful and popular. Unicorns are very rare," she added in a superior tone, "like the mythical creature we're named for."

"Janet's really laying it on thick," Mary whispered to Jessica with a grin.

"I guess she wants to make sure that Brooke gets the right idea about us," Jessica whispered back.

"And of course," Janet was saying grandly, "we only invite the most special girls to be members of the Unicorns. They have to be girls we can count on to uphold the Unicorn image. That's why we've invited you this afternoon, Brooke.''

Brooke looked around. "I see," she said.

"What Janet is trying to say," Lila put in impatiently, "is that we're inviting you to be a Unicorn."

"Of course," Janet said, "this is only a preliminary invitation. First you have to complete your pledge task. Then we'll vote on whether to let you into the club."

"Pledge task?" Brooke asked.

"Every Unicorn has to perform a certain task that is assigned to her." Janet turned to Jessica. "Jessica, has the committee decided on a pledge task for Brooke?"

"We haven't come up with one yet," Jessica admitted, feeling a little embarrassed. "We're still working on it. We want it to be exactly right for Brooke."

Janet nodded and turned back to Brooke. "When the committee has decided on your pledge task, you'll have a day or two to carry it out. Then the committee will report on how well you did, and we'll all take a vote. What do you say, Brooke?"

Brooke hesitated. "I . . . I don't know exactly what to say."

"I can understand that," Ellen said reassuringly. "It's a big responsibility to be a Unicorn."

"What exactly do Unicorns do?" Brooke asked.

Everybody looked at Janet.

"We hold meetings, of course," she said. "Wednesday is our regular meeting day. You're expected to attend every week, unless you have a really good excuse. And we give parties."

"What else do you do?" Brooke prodded.

There was silence.

"We get together and go shopping," Lila said at last.

"And once we sold celebrity cookbooks," Mary added.

"Yes," Lila concurred triumphantly. "We do lots of different things."

"I guess I'll have to think about it for a day or two," Brooke said slowly. "I can see that Ellen is right. It's a very big responsibility to be a Unicorn. I'm not sure I'm ready for it."

Janet stared at her. "You're not sure? But I thought Lila said that you *wanted* to be a Unicorn."

At that moment, the doorbell rang and Jessica hurried to answer it. A postman handed her a big fat envelope. "Special delivery for Miss Jessica Wakefield," he said as he thrust a clipboard at her. "Sign on the line, please."

Jessica signed her name and then carried her envelope back into the den. She was looking at it in a puzzled way when Mary came over to her.

"What is it, Jessica?" she asked.

"I don't know," Jessica said. She turned the envelope over.

"*Teenager Magazine*," Ellen read over Jessica's shoulder. "Did you order something from *Teenager Magazine*?"

"No," Jessica said, "not that I remember." And then, she *did* remember. She'd entered that contest!

"Well," Lila asked, "aren't you going to open it?"

Jessica's stomach suddenly felt queasy. "Not now," she said. "I think I'll open it later."

"Don't be silly, Jessica," Janet said. "It came special delivery. That means it's important. You have to open it right away."

So, with everybody standing around looking at her, Jessica opened the envelope. There was a letter inside, along with several other pieces of paper. As Jessica opened the letter, she felt her face go pale.

"Well, read it," Janet commanded insistently.

"Congratulations, Mademoiselle Wakefield," Jessica read out loud, in an unsteady voice.

"*Mademoiselle* Wakefield?" Kimberly repeated with a laugh.

"Be quiet, Kimberly," Janet said sternly.

"Go on, Jessica. Read the rest of it. It sounds as if you might have won something."

Jessica took a deep breath and continued to read. "You and your outstanding French-oriented family have been selected as finalists in our Model Family contest. You are eligible to win a week-long trip to Paris. One of our local representatives will contact you in the next few days to set up a visit with you and your family. Good luck!"

For a few seconds, there was silence. Then Mary said, in an awestruck voice, "A week in Paris! Wow, Jessica, that's *fantastic*! How lucky can you get?"

Ellen gave her a hug. "That's terrific, Jessica! I am *so* jealous!"

"We haven't won the contest," Jessica said numbly. "We're just finalists."

How did it happen? she asked herself. Couldn't the judges see that she'd just made all that stuff up about her perfect family? Jessica reread the letter. A representative was coming to see the family. She didn't remember anything about that in the contest rules. What was she going to do when the representative showed up and found out that she had lied on the entry form? She would be humiliated.

But right now, everybody was congratulating her. And everybody was very excited, everybody but Lila, who looked as if she just didn't see what all the fuss was about.

"You're going to win!" Kimberly said, dancing up and down. "I know it, I know it!"

"You've *got* to win, Jessica," Betsy added, "for the honor of the Unicorns."

"Yes," Janet said thoughtfully, "Betsy's right. If you win this contest, it will be a terrific reflection on the Unicorns. You've to give it all you've got, Jessica."

"That's right," Tamara said. "The Unicorns can't afford for you to fail, Jessica. You've *got* to win!"

"You see how wonderful it is to be a Unicorn, Brooke?" Ellen said happily. "We all stand behind one another. One for all and all for one!"

"Right," Kimberly agreed. "And you can see that the Unicorns are so special they're even recognized by a national magazine. When Jessica wins this contest, her picture will be *everywhere!*"

Brooke noticed that not one of the Unicorns had commented on the French-oriented aspect of the contest. "I didn't know that your family was interested in French things, Jessica. *Parlez-vous français?*" she asked.

Jessica put the package on the coffee table without answering Brooke. "Hey, you guys," she said, looking around, "I haven't won anything yet, and I'd really like to surprise my family. So, uh, please don't say anything about this to anybody, OK?''

"Surprise them?" Brooke asked. "You mean, your family doesn't know anything about this contest?"

"How about some more refreshments, everybody?" Jessica asked quickly.

"Yes, have another cookie, Brooke," Lila said, "and let me tell you some more about the Unicorns."

For Jessica, the party seemed to go on forever. When it was finally over and everyone had left, Jessica hurriedly dug through the envelope and found a copy of the contest rules. Because they were mostly in fine print, Jessica borrowed her father's magnifying glass from his desk drawer. She skimmed the sheet until she found the place where it said that finalists would be visited by a representative of the magazine. The representatives would help pick the first-prize winner.

Jessica sat back and tried to figure out what to do. The honorable thing, she knew, would be to let the contest officials know that she wrote the essay for fun and that her sister had mailed it by mistake.

The doorbell rang again. It was Lila.

"I forgot my notebook," she said.

Jessica led Lila down the hall. "It's probably

in the den," she said. The girls found it lying on the floor where Lila had been sitting.

"I see that you're going over the contest information," Lila said with a glance at the papers Jessica had been reading. She lifted her chin. "I really don't know what everyone was so excited about, Jessica. I doubt you'll win."

Jessica bristled. "Why?" she asked.

"Because there'll be so many really *good* finalists," Lila said loftily. "Your family doesn't stand a chance of winning that trip to Paris. Now, if it were *my* family, it would be a different story. My father—"

All of Jessica's resentment came rushing back in a hot flood. Lila was always thinking that her family was better than everybody else's!

"Well, I think you're wrong," Jessica interrupted angrily. "We've got as good a chance of winning as anybody, maybe better. And I'll *prove* it." And she would, too. Maybe she had entered the contest by accident. But now she and her family were finalists, and she was determined to win that trip to Paris. She would show Lila!

But when Lila was gone, Jessica's determination began to fade. Winning the contest was going to be very difficult, considering the fact that her family wasn't really interested in France. And considering that her contest application was almost entirely fictional.

Five

◇

Elizabeth smiled to herself and hummed a little as she walked home from Amy's later that afternoon. She and Amy had been to the park where they had seen Todd and Amy's friend Ken Matthews. They'd played a quick game of basketball together and had had a lot of fun.

A block from home, Elizabeth ran into Brooke.

"Hi, Brooke." Elizabeth looked at her curiously. She'd been wondering how Brooke was doing with the Unicorns and whether she would change her mind and join them. "How was the party?" she asked.

Brooke smiled. "Todd was right after all. They *did* ask me to join. Jessica's on a committee to figure out my pledge task. If they like the way I perform the task, they'll vote me in."

"So you've decided to be a Unicorn?" Elizabeth asked.

Brooke shook her head. "I didn't tell them one way or the other. I just said that being a Unicorn was a huge responsibility, and I wasn't sure I was ready for it. I sort of left things up in the air."

Elizabeth grinned. "I'll bet that surprised them."

"Well, Lila looked surprised, anyway," Brooke agreed. "I guess she expected me to jump up and down and rush right out and buy a whole closetful of purple clothes." She looked carefully at Elizabeth. "I think you're right when you call the Unicorns the Snob Squad, Elizabeth. Some of the girls are nice, but a lot of them are pretty stuck on themselves. But you were wrong about the meeting being boring."

"I was?" Elizabeth asked in surprise. "You mean, they didn't talk just about clothes and boys?"

"Janet complimented me on my outfit," Brooke replied, "but we never got around to the subject of boys. Everybody was too excited about Jessica's letter. After it came, that was all everyone talked about."

"Jessica's letter?" *What is Jessica up to now?* Elizabeth wondered.

"It came special delivery, right in the middle of the meeting," Brooke said.

"Special delivery?" Elizabeth raised her eyebrows. "Then it must have been pretty important. Who could have sent her a special delivery letter?"

Brooke hesitated. "Well, Jessica didn't want your family to find out about it just yet, so she asked the Unicorns not to tell you. But I'm a little concerned, Elizabeth. I think Jessica might be in over her head."

Elizabeth laughed a little. "Jessica gets in over her head at least once a week. What's it all about anyway?"

"Well, it seems that you and your family are finalists in a contest," Brooke explained. "The prize is an all-expense-paid trip to Paris."

"A trip to *Paris*?" Elizabeth was flabbergasted. "What kind of contest is it?"

"I don't know all the details," Brooke replied, "but Jessica read her letter of congratulations to us. It said that the contest is being held to pick an outstanding French-oriented American family."

Elizabeth laughed. "French-oriented family? Well, that leaves us out, for sure. I can't believe we're even qualified to be in the contest. I wonder how we got to be finalists?"

"Do any of you speak French?" Brooke asked.

"I don't, and neither does Jessica," Elizabeth said. "All the French words we know we've learned in Madame Andre's ballet class. Mom and Dad may have studied French in college, but even if they did, that was a long time ago. I doubt they remember much." She shook her head. "I can't understand why Jessica would have entered us in a contest like that, Brooke. I'll have to ask her."

"Well, you'd better ask her soon," Brooke told her. "The letter said that a representative from the contest will contact your family in a few days to set up a visit."

"Uh-oh." Elizabeth sighed. "This is beginning to sound serious. I'd better talk to her this afternoon."

"You can say I told you, if you want." Brooke frowned. "I hope she won't be upset with me for telling."

"I hope so, too," Elizabeth said. "But it sounds like something I should know about."

Elizabeth's mother was in the kitchen preparing dinner when Elizabeth got home. "Hi, Mom," Elizabeth greeted her. "Where's Jessica?"

"She rode her bike to the library to do some research," Mrs. Wakefield replied.

"Research?" Elizabeth asked in surprise.

"It has something to do with France," Mrs.

Wakefield said, opening the refrigerator. "I think it's for a class project."

"Maybe," Elizabeth said doubtfully. *It probably has something to do with the contest*, she thought.

Mrs. Wakefield looked up with a smile. "You know, your sister does have some serious interests, Elizabeth. She isn't as scatter-brained as she acts sometimes."

"I know," Elizabeth said. But she was thinking that Jessica's main interest right now probably wasn't one that her mother would approve of. She looked around the kitchen. "Can I help you with dinner, Mom?"

"I think I've got everything under control here, honey," Mrs. Wakefield said, putting a bowl of lettuce and some carrots on the counter. "By the way, Elizabeth, how do you and Jessica feel about Dynamo? Do you like their music?"

Elizabeth laughed. "*Like* it?" she asked. "Dynamo is terrific! I'm still hoping you actually get to meet Nick England, and not just talk to him on the phone about your plans for his parents' house. And Jessica would probably trade her Johnny Buck poster for good tickets to Dynamo's concert." She looked at her mother curiously. "Why?"

"Oh, no reason," Mrs. Wakefield said with a little smile. "And if you haven't already, I wouldn't mention to Jessica the fact that I'm doing a project for Nick England. You know how crazy she gets over rock stars. I wouldn't want her to get her hopes up about meeting him someday."

"OK, Mom. I guess I'll get started on my homework." Elizabeth went upstairs to her room. She had barely started her math homework when she heard Jessica come barreling up the stairs. Elizabeth closed her book and started toward Jessica's room. When she reached the doorway, she saw Jessica sitting on her bed, leafing through a Paris guidebook.

"Hi, Jessica." Elizabeth glanced at the book. "Planning a trip to Paris?"

Hurriedly, Jessica put the guidebook behind her. "Uh, no," she said. "I . . . I've got to do some research for a . . . a school report, that's all."

Elizabeth looked steadily at her sister. "Your 'research' wouldn't have anything to do with a contest, would it?"

Jessica lifted her chin. "Contest?" she asked, looking innocently at her sister. "What contest?"

"Jessica," Elizabeth said, "you know what I'm talking about. Brooke told me about the special delivery letter you got this afternoon."

"Brooke?" Jessica frowned. "But I told everybody not to tell!" She colored guiltily. "I mean, I asked them not to tell you just yet. I wanted it to be a surprise."

"It's a surprise, all right," Elizabeth said. "Why did you enter us in a contest like that? We don't even qualify."

Jessica looked down at the floor. "Actually," she muttered, "I didn't enter the contest."

"Then how did we get to be finalists?" Elizabeth persisted.

"I didn't enter the contest," Jessica repeated. "*You* did."

"Me?" Elizabeth laughed. "That's ridiculous, Jessica."

"But I'm serious, Elizabeth!" Jessica cried. "Remember that envelope you put in the mail for me? Well, that was the contest entry form. You sent it to *Teenager Magazine*."

"I did?" Elizabeth asked, as she tried to remember. "I guess maybe I did. But if you didn't mean to send in the entry form, why did you fill it out?"

Jessica blushed. "I was just playing around."

"Playing around? With an *official contest*?"

Jessica's blue-green eyes filled with tears. "Don't be so hard on me, Lizzie. I didn't mean to do anything wrong. I was just so sick of Lila's stories, and of not having anything to brag about myself. So when I saw the contest entry form, I wrote down a bunch of really good stuff about us—about Steven and you and me and Mom and Dad—to make myself feel better. I didn't actually mean to send it in."

"Really good stuff?" Elizabeth asked, narrowing her eyes. "What kind of really good stuff?"

Jessica shrugged. "Oh, I didn't say much, really. I just told them that Mom was a good cook, and that Dad liked to paint—"

"Dad doesn't paint!"

"Well, he does a little," Jessica defended. "He painted the end table in the den, didn't he? And I told them about Steven's trombone."

Elizabeth laughed. "I don't see how Steven's trombone playing could help anybody win a contest. Unless it's a contest for the worst trombone player in history. He's pretty terrible."

"The contest people don't know that," Jessica said in a low voice.

"But they will when the representative comes to visit us," Elizabeth pointed out.

Jessica bit her lip. "So you know about that, too?"

Elizabeth nodded. "When is she supposed to come?"

"I don't know. Soon, I guess. The letter said she would contact us," Jessica answered.

Elizabeth sat down on the bed. "Listen, Jess," she said earnestly, "you've got to call the magazine and tell them you entered the contest by mistake. Nobody in our family has any interest in *anything* French. There's no way we could compete in a contest like that."

Jessica swallowed. "But it sounds so dumb to tell them that I didn't mean to enter the contest. There's got to be another way, Elizabeth."

Elizabeth shook her head. "If there is, I can't think of it. You have to come clean, Jess. If you don't, Mom and Dad will have a fit."

"Elizabeth, you aren't going to tell them, are you?" Jessica pleaded. "At least wait until I get this worked out. Anyway, wouldn't it be fun if we all won a free trip to Paris? Wouldn't you like to go?"

"Of course I'd like to go," Elizabeth exclaimed. "But there's no way we can win that trip, Jessica. Whatever you said on the entry form that made them pick us for finalists couldn't possibly have been true."

"Maybe not all of it," Jessica admitted. "I can't remember everything I said. But our family *is* close to perfect, Elizabeth," she added earnestly. "There are lots of interesting things about us. I think we might stand a chance in the contest, if we give it a try."

Elizabeth laughed. "Maybe we *are* a model family. But we're not the kind of model family the magazine is looking for. They want a family that has French interests."

"Anyway," Jessica went on, ignoring Elizabeth's remark, "I don't want to back down in front of Lila. I hate the way she's always going on about her father and about how he's so rich and how he always gives her everything she asks for." She frowned. "Our family is every bit as wonderful as Lila's. And this contest gives me the chance to prove it to Lila and to everybody else."

Elizabeth shook her head. "I know how you feel about Lila, Jess. But there's just no way we can compete in the contest. It's a lost cause. And Mom and Dad would never agree to go along with it. You've got to tell the truth. And *right away*, too."

"All right. I'll take care of it, Elizabeth," Jessica said with a sigh.

Elizabeth looked at her twin. "You'll call the magazine and tell them that we're pulling out of the contest?"

"I'll take care of it," Jessica repeated. *And I will, too*, she promised herself as Elizabeth left the room. *As soon as I figure out how.*

When dinner was over that evening, Steven jumped up from the table. "How about if I help with the dishes?" he asked.

Mrs. Wakefield stared at her son. "Are you feeling all right, Steven?"

Mr. Wakefield blinked. "Are you sure this person is our son? The Steven I know would never volunteer for kitchen chores. This guy must be an imposter."

Elizabeth laughed as Steven sighed. "You guys never give me any credit," he complained.

"That's because you don't deserve any credit," Jessica remarked, helping herself to a second piece of pie. "The only reason you're offering to help in the kitchen is because you don't want to practice your trombone."

Steven glared at his sister. "Did anybody ask your opinion?" he growled.

"Tell you what, Steven," Mr. Wakefield said cheerfully, standing up. "How about the two of us giving the women a break this evening? We'll handle the kitchen for a change. When we're finished, you can get right to your trombone. I know you don't want to miss a single second of your practice."

"Terrific," Steven muttered, with another dark look at Jessica. He picked up a dirty dish. "Jessica, when you've finished shoveling that pie down, would you bring your plate to the kitchen?"

Jessica scowled at him. She couldn't come up with a creative retort just now because she was still thinking about the contest and worrying about what she was going to do. Usually, when she got into trouble, it wasn't too hard to think of a way to bail herself out. But this time, the whole family was involved. If she came up with any kind of solution, she was going to have to convince four other people—Steven, Elizabeth, and her parents—to cooperate. And that wasn't going to be easy. In fact, it was going to be very difficult. Her mom and dad would probably tell her just what Elizabeth had told her, to call the magazine and withdraw from the contest.

But just as Jessica had almost convinced herself that it was ridiculous, even to try to get her family's cooperation, she remembered Lila. If she pulled out of the contest, she would be humiliated in front of the entire Unicorn Club and Lila would never let her hear the end of it. What could she do? There didn't seem to be any solution.

A half hour later, Jessica was lying upstairs on her bed, still trying to come up with an answer. But she wasn't having much luck, because Steven was practicing his trombone. Even though he was down in the basement, he could be heard through the entire house, and he was awful. Jessica was just considering stuffing some cotton in her ears, when the phone rang.

"I'll get it!" Jessica yelled as she sprang up. Maybe it was one of the Unicorns. She was tired of thinking about the contest.

Out in the hall, Jessica picked up the phone. "Hello."

"*Puis-je parler à Mademoiselle Wakefield, s'il*

vous plaît?" a voice said in rapid French. The words *Mademoiselle Wakefield* were the only words Jessica recognized.

Jessica gulped. "This is me," she said. "I mean, this is Jessica Wakefield."

"Je m'appelle Marie Harris," the woman replied, still speaking in French. "I represent *Teenager Magazine*. I am calling from our office in San Francisco about the contest."

"Uh, there's a lot of noise on my end," Jessica stammered. "I couldn't quite hear what you said." The part about the noise was true. Steven's trombone was blaring.

The woman spoke more loudly. "My name is Marie Harris," she said, this time in English. "I represent *Teenager Magazine*. I am calling about the contest you've entered. Our judges were very impressed by your family's many achievements. Congratulations on becoming a finalist!"

"Oh," Jessica said. "Thank you. Uh, I was just thinking of calling you to ask whether—"

"Then I have saved you a phone call," Ms. Harris said pleasantly. "I'll be in Sweet Valley on Thursday evening. Would that be a convenient time for me to drop in on your family for a couple of hours? I was thinking that perhaps we could have dinner, so that I could sample some of your mother's French cooking. I'd love to see some of your father's paintings, too, and hear your brother play his trombone."

Down in the basement, Steven let out a blast that nearly shook the walls. Jessica pulled the phone into her room and closed the door. "Thursday?" she asked, feeling panicked. "Do you mean *this* Thursday?" Today was Monday!

"Perhaps we could schedule it for Wednesday," Ms. Harris said. "Or even tomorrow."

"Oh, no," Jessica said quickly. "Thursday would be much better."

"I know that this is short notice," Ms. Harris said, "but we planned it this way so that the finalist families wouldn't go to a lot of trouble to get ready for our visit. Please tell your family not to do anything special just because I'll be there looking on and taking notes. Just treat me as if I were one of the family."

"We will." Jessica couldn't think of anything else to say.

"Well, then," Ms. Harris said briskly, "it is decided. Thursday evening, shall we say, seven o'clock?"

"*Très bien*," Jessica said, summoning the little French she could remember from Madame Andre's ballet class. "*Au revoir*."

"*Au revoir*, Mademoiselle Wakefield," Ms. Harris said, sounding pleased. "Until Thursday at seven."

As Jessica put the phone down, another blast from Steven's trombone rattled the walls.

Six

◇

Now Jessica really had to come up with a plan.
For what seemed like hours that Monday night
she wracked her brain. It was impossible to pull
out of the contest now, so she had to think of
a way to talk her family into cooperating when
Ms. Harris came by on Thursday night. After
what seemed like an eternity, she finally came
up with a terrific plan, the best she'd ever
concocted.

The only problem with this terrific plan was
that she needed her entire family's cooperation
to pull it off. As she got dressed for school on
Tuesday morning, Jessica grinned at herself in
the mirror, trying to quiet the butterflies in her
stomach. *If I can pull this off*, she told herself,
there isn't anything I can't do!

Downstairs in the kitchen, the family was gathered for breakfast. Mr. Wakefield was reading his paper and drinking a cup of coffee. Steven was digging into his cereal, and Elizabeth was pouring orange juice while Mrs. Wakefield dished up the scrambled eggs. She was telling the family about her new client.

"I'm very excited about this project," she was saying. "It isn't often that you get to work with a client like—"

"Hi, everybody." Jessica burst into the room with her most dazzling smile. "Want me to make the toast?"

"Why, thank you, Jessica," Mrs. Wakefield said.

Jessica put four slices of bread into the toaster. "I've got some wonderful news!" she announced.

"The Unicorns have declared themselves extinct?" Steven asked between mouthfuls.

"Steven," Jessica said reproachfully. She looked at her mother. "It's terrific news, really. It's about a trip. A really *wonderful* trip. The trip of a lifetime." She poured her cereal into a bowl and added milk.

Elizabeth looked carefully at Jessica, but didn't say anything.

"A trip?" Mrs. Wakefield asked, putting a jar of jam on the table. "Where to, Jessica?"

"To Paris!" Jessica said excitedly. "And we

can all go! It's a trip for the whole family. A *week-long* trip."

Mr. Wakefield lowered his paper. "Sorry to disappoint you, Jessica, but we can't go. A trip to Paris for five people would cost a fortune."

Those were exactly the words Jessica had been waiting for. "But it's *free!*" she announced dramatically. "We *won* it! Well, almost," she added, as the toast popped up. "We just have to do one or two things, that's all."

Mrs. Wakefield sat down at the table. "A free trip? Jessica, what are you talking about?"

"I entered a contest," Jessica explained, buttering a piece of toast. "Actually, though, it wasn't me. I mean, I didn't do it alone. All I did was write an essay about what a terrific family we are. Elizabeth entered the contest." She gave Elizabeth a warm smile and handed her the toast. "We can thank *her* for our trip to Paris."

"Just a minute, Jessica," Elizabeth protested. "I didn't have anything to do with—"

"And yesterday," Jessica went on smoothly, "I got a special delivery letter saying that we're finalists in the contest. All we have to do is have an interview with the magazine's representative, Ms. Harris." She put all the enthusiasm that she could muster into her voice. "And then we can pack our bags for Paris!"

Steven looked thoughtful. "Paris, huh? I've

always wanted to see the Eiffel Tower. And I hear that French girls are really something.''

Elizabeth leaned forward. ''It isn't quite as simple as that, is it, Jessica?'' she asked with a meaningful glance. ''There must be more to it.''

Jessica took a few bites of her cereal. ''Well, maybe,'' she admitted. ''I mean, we *will* have to make a little extra effort for the interviewer.''

''This interview,'' Mr. Wakefield said. ''What's it about?''

''It's about . . .'' Jessica hesitated. This was the hard part. She took a deep breath. ''Well, it's about how interested we are in France,'' she said. ''You see, they're looking for the model French-oriented family.''

Mr. Wakefield picked up his paper again. ''Well, you can forget about Paris,'' he said with a laugh. ''Our interest in France would just about fill a thimble.'' He grinned at Mrs. Wakefield. ''Do you remember any of your French, Alice?''

''I'm afraid not,'' Mrs. Wakefield said regretfully. ''The last time I studied French was back in high school.'' She looked at Jessica. ''Jessica, whatever made you enter a contest like that? And what did you say about us that got us all the way to the finals?''

''You must have laid it on pretty thick.'' Steven grinned. ''I'll bet you told them some real whoppers.''

"I did not," Jessica defended herself. She paused. "Well, I have to admit that I stretched things a little, but not much." She looked at her mother. "For instance, I told them that you were a good cook, and that you liked to cook French dishes."

Mrs. Wakefield laughed. "If you're thinking of my French Apple Pie, forget it. It came straight out of the *Pies of the World Cookbook*. I'm afraid you've been exaggerating again, Jessica."

"But you're still a good cook," Jessica insisted. "I'll bet you could cook something really French." She paused. "I, um, also said that you're a ballet dancer."

Mrs. Wakefield looked surprised. "I had a few lessons when I was a girl. But that was a long time ago, and I never even got up on my toes. Why couldn't you have told them about something I'm really good at, Jessica?"

Jessica blushed and looked at her father. "And you're a good painter," she added. "That's what I told them about you."

"I did do a pretty good job on that end table," Mr. Wakefield said modestly. "But I hardly think that has anything to do with French—"

"No, I mean, *oil* painting." Jessica put on a contrite look. "That's probably where I stretched things the most."

Mr. Wakefield looked at her sternly. "And just what else did you say about me, Jessica?"

"That you're a famous artist," Jessica said in a small voice. "That you have a studio at home and that your paintings are in the local galleries."

Mr. Wakefield hooted. "Jessica, you certainly have a wild imagination!"

Jessica turned quickly to Steven. "I really said some good things about you, Steven," she went on in a flattering voice. "I told them that you're a neat big brother and a star basketball player—"

"Yeah, well, *that's* the truth, anyway," Steven said thoughtfully.

"—and I told them that you play the trombone—"

Steven put down his spoon.

"—so well that you have your own jazz ensemble," Jessica finished lamely.

"Wow, what a dreamer," Steven said, shaking his head. "Jessica, where did you come up with all this stuff? A French cook and ballet dancer, a famous artist, a jazz trombonist." He grinned. "What did you tell them about Elizabeth?"

"I . . . I couldn't think of anything to make her sound any better than she already is," Jessica said. "So I just told the truth."

"Congratulations, Liz," Steven said with a

grin. "You're so terrific that even Jessica can't improve on you." He turned to Jessica. "And what did you say about yourself?"

Jessica shrugged. "Oh, not much," she said. "I just told them that Elizabeth and I are a lot alike."

Steven laughed so hard he almost fell off his chair. "I've got to hand it to you, Jessica, you've really outdone yourself this time. But, I think it's a fiction contest you should have entered."

Even Elizabeth had to smile at that, and Mr. Wakefield was obviously making an effort to look stern. "The best thing for you to do, Jessica," he said, "is to call the magazine and tell them that it was all a big mistake. We don't have any business competing in a contest like this one."

"But Dad," Jessica pleaded, "I'm not asking for much. All you have to do is go along with me for just a couple of hours while Ms. Harris is here."

"When is she supposed to come?" Mrs. Wakefield asked thoughtfully.

"On Thursday," Jessica said. "I know it's short notice, but she said they plan it that way so the finalists won't go to any special trouble. She wants to see us just the way we are." She paused, looking at them anxiously. "I mean, just the way I described us."

Mrs. Wakefield laughed a little. "I suppose that means I'd have to cook a French dinner, and your father would have to show off his paintings, and Steven would have to put on a trombone performance. Is that it?"

"Well, you wouldn't have to actually *do* any of those things," Jessica said hesitantly. "You could just talk about them. Oh, and there's one more thing."

Mrs. Wakefield sighed. "What is it?"

"We'd all have to speak a little French," Jessica said.

"Speak *French?*" Steven shouted and burst into laughter again.

"Don't you think that would be a little difficult?" Mrs. Wakefield asked mildly. "Particularly since none of us knows any French."

"But we all know a few French words," Jessica replied quickly. "Like *merci beaucoup* and *au revoir*. We could just sort of sprinkle them here and there in the conversation, couldn't we?"

"Really, Jessica," Mr. Wakefield said, shaking his head, "this nonsense has gone far enough. Let's not talk anymore about it. Just get on the phone and . . ."

"You mean, you really don't want to go to Paris, Ned?" Mrs. Wakefield asked. "It's something I know I've always wanted to do."

Jessica looked up quickly. It sounded as if her mother were on her side!

Mr. Wakefield stared at his wife. "Go to Paris? Alice, there's not a chance in the world that we could win that contest. Jessica has completely misrepresented us."

Mrs. Wakefield looked thoughtful. "Well, not completely. I admit that she's stretched the truth a bit—"

"Stretched it a *bit?*" Steven snorted. "If the truth were a rubber band, it would have popped by now!"

"—but she hasn't said anything all that outrageous," Mrs. Wakefield continued, with a frown at Steven.

Jessica leaned forward eagerly. "Really, Dad," she said, "you wouldn't have to do very much. I mean, you don't actually have to show Ms. Harris any paintings. You could just sort of mention them."

"That's right, Ned," Mrs. Wakefield put in. "You could just sort of, well, throw painting into the conversation, along with a few French words. You know, like *bon voyage* and *parlez-vous française* and so on."

Jessica was amazed at the way her mother was standing up for her. It was almost too good to be true. Her father seemed to be amazed, too. He was looking at his wife with a bewildered expression. Even Steven and Elizabeth were speechless.

"Then you'll do it?" Jessica asked happily. "You'll try to win the contest?"

"We'll do it," Mrs. Wakefield confirmed. "I'll start thinking about a special French dish I can make. And I'll look up a few ballet terms in the dictionary."

"Mom, that's terrific!" Jessica cried, amazed at how easy it had been to convince her family to go along with her plan. If the rest of it went this well, they'd be in Paris before she could say *bon voyage*. She gobbled the last bit of her cereal and pushed her chair back. "Listen, I've got to get to school," she said. "I've got some important things to do."

As the door slammed behind Jessica, Elizabeth looked at her mother. *She must have something up her sleeve*, she thought. *But what?*

Mr. Wakefield turned to his wife. "Alice," he said very quietly, "what do you mean by encouraging Jessica? She should call that magazine and tell them that this whole thing was a product of her overactive imagination."

Mrs. Wakefield nodded. "She probably should, Ned. But that would be the easy way out. If we make Jessica do that, she won't learn anything."

"Learn anything?" Elizabeth repeated curiously.

"I think Jessica needs to be taught a lesson about exaggeration," Mrs. Wakefield said firmly.

"And Thursday evening will be the perfect time to teach her."

"Just what did you have in mind, Alice?" Mr. Wakefield asked.

"I thought we might just do a little exaggerating ourselves," Mrs. Wakefield replied with a smile, "although we probably won't exactly be the model French-oriented family that Jessica has in mind."

Elizabeth giggled. "This could be fun."

"It sure could," Steven said. "I wonder what that representative will think of my trombone playing. For the right audience, I think I could get into the mood to give a concert."

Mr. Wakefield grinned. "You know, I've always admired Matisse. He was a pretty colorful character."

"That's the spirit," Mrs. Wakefield said. "But it would probably be a good idea to let Ms. Harris know what happened and clue her in on our plan. I think I'll give the magazine a call this morning. If Ms. Harris is willing to go along with us, I think we have an interesting evening ahead."

Jessica could hardly wait for lunch that day to put the rest of her plan into action. When Ellen and Mary joined her at the Unicorner, she started to work immediately.

"I've thought of the most terrific idea for

Brooke's pledge task," she said. "It fits Brooke perfectly."

"I'm glad you've come up with something," Mary said. "I couldn't think of anything really good."

"What is it?" Ellen asked.

Jessica leaned forward. "You know that contest my family is in, to find the model French-oriented family? Well, the representative from *Teenager Magazine* is coming to dinner on Thursday."

"So?" Ellen took a bite of her pizza. "What does that have to do with Brooke's pledge task?"

"We're going to have a French dinner for the representative," Jessica explained. "My mother is going to cook a special French dish and—" Jessica didn't really want to tell them the rest of it. "Brooke's task will be to dress up in a French maid's uniform and serve dinner. It'll be perfect for her."

"You're right, it would," Mary said. "She could even speak French. She spent a summer in Paris."

Ellen looked doubtful. "It's a good idea. But our other pledge tasks have all taken place at school or someplace where at least a few Unicorns could witness them," she said. "If Brooke performs her task at your house, you're the only one who'll be there to see it."

Jessica had already thought of that. "You and Mary could come and peek through the dining room window," she suggested. "Lila could come too. After all, she's the one who suggested Brooke for membership."

"I don't think I can come Thursday night," Mary said.

"I can," Ellen said. "I'll ask Lila if she wants to come with me."

Jessica smiled happily. Everything was working out beautifully. Ms. Harris would be impressed by the fact that the Wakefields had a French maid. Lila would be impressed by the fact that Jessica was having dinner with a representative from *Teenager Magazine*. And if everything went according to plan, the Wakefields stood a good chance of winning the trip to Paris. That would impress Lila even more.

It was a perfect plan!

Seven

◇

After school on Tuesday, Jessica hurried to Brooke's locker. Brooke was just putting her books away when Jessica found her.

"Hi, Brooke," Jessica said breathlessly. "Listen, the committee has met and we've decided . . ."

"The committee?" Brooke asked. "What committee?"

Jessica was shocked. Had Brooke forgotten about her Unicorn initiation? Had she decided she didn't want to join the club after all? She had to do the pledge task! It was essential to the success of Jessica's plan.

"The committee that's deciding on your pledge task, of course," Jessica said. "I hope you haven't forgotten."

Brooke laughed easily. "Oh, that. Sorry, Jessica. No, I hadn't forgotten. I've just been really busy today, and it slipped my mind. What am I supposed to do?"

Jessica felt relieved. "It's a really special task," she said. "But it isn't hard, and it's something you probably won't mind doing at all. It'll even be fun. And it's perfect for you."

"Really? What is it?"

"On Thursday evening, you have to dress up in a French maid's uniform—"

Brooke raised her eyebrows. "A French *maid's* uniform?"

"It's a black dress with a short skirt and a starched white apron," Jessica explained. "And a white cap, if you can get it." She hesitated. Maybe it wouldn't be easy to find an outfit like that.

"I can probably get a maid's uniform at the costume rental store," Brooke said, "although I'm not sure that a French maid looks any different from any other maid. What am I supposed to do when I'm dressed up in it?"

Jessica frowned. Brooke sounded a little too amused for her liking. "You don't have to do very much," she said. "Just come to my house at seven and serve dinner, that's all. Or," she hesitated, "maybe it would be better if you came at six-thirty. That way you could help my mother with the cooking."

"Serve dinner? Help with the cooking?" Brooke sounded surprised.

"That's right," Jessica said firmly. "And while you're serving, it would be very helpful if you spoke a little French. You don't have to say a lot. Just drop a few French words into the conversation while you're bringing in the food and clearing up."

Brooke cleared her throat. "You wouldn't by any chance be having a guest, would you? Somebody from *Teenager Magazine*?"

Jessica looked at her quickly. "Did Elizabeth tell you that?"

Brooke shook her head. "Just a lucky guess. OK, Jessica. You can count on me. I'll be there on Thursday evening at six-thirty. Oh, by the way, I can talk to Elizabeth about this, can't I?"

Jessica hesitated. Usually the Unicorn initiations were supposed to be top secret. But Elizabeth would be at the dinner, so there was no point in trying to keep Brooke's pledge task from her twin.

"Sure," Jessica said. "Just don't talk about it with anybody else. OK?"

"OK." Brooke closed her locker and slung her book bag over her shoulder.

"By the way," Jessica said, "there's one more thing. Since you'll be speaking a little French, I wonder if you'd mind using a French name for the evening. Like Brookette."

Brooke stared at her. *"Brookette?"*

Jessica nodded. "It sounds very French, don't you think?" Without waiting for an answer, she went on, "I'm meeting Lila and Ellen at the Dairi Burger in a few minutes. Want to come along?"

"Thanks," Brooke said, "but I've already made other plans. Maybe another time."

"OK," Jessica said. "Don't forget, Thursday night at six-thirty."

Jessica practically skipped to the Dairi Burger. Things were working out perfectly! It had been a stroke of genius to think of having a French maid at dinner. Ms. Harris would be very impressed.

Jessica smiled ecstatically. She could see herself strolling down the beautiful Parisian streets and posing for a snapshot in front of the Eiffel Tower. When she got back, she'd be the envy of Sweet Valley Middle School.

Lila and Ellen were already at the Dairi Burger, drinking sodas.

"Well?" Ellen demanded as Jessica slid into the booth. "Did Brooke say yes?"

Jessica nodded happily. "She'll be at my house at six-thirty. She's going to help with the cooking, too."

"This is a pretty unusual pledge task," Lila remarked. "Why couldn't you come up with something for her to do at school?"

Jessica had been expecting that question. "Because I wanted something original for Brooke," she explained. "You know, something that would let her be creative. The French dinner we're having for the representative of *Teenager Magazine* was a good opportunity."

"I think it's a cute task, Lila," Ellen said. "It's different."

"Well, I guess," Lila said grudgingly. "But I refuse to peep through a window, Jessica. That's so childish."

Jessica was disappointed. She'd counted on Lila seeing how well the dinner was going. "Don't you think that some other Unicorns ought to witness her task?" she asked, hoping to change Lila's mind.

Lila thought for a minute. "OK, here's what we'll do. Ellen and I will drop by your house sometime Thursday evening to see how things are going."

"Well, OK." Jessica agreed. She would have to be satisfied with that. She couldn't wait for Lila to see her model family in action, winning the trip to Paris!

"Jessica asked you to do *what*?" Elizabeth stared at Brooke in disbelief.

Brooke bent over to tie the lace on her rollerskate. "To dress up like a French maid," she repeated, "and serve dinner at your house on

Thursday evening. My name is supposed to be Brookette."

"*Brookette?*" Elizabeth asked with a grin.

Brooke straightened up. "I thought it was kind of a weird pledge task, but I didn't tell her that."

Elizabeth burst out laughing as the two girls began to skate. "Sometimes I can't believe the crazy ideas Jessica comes up with," she said. "It's hard to be mad at her, even when she pulls something like this."

"Was I right? Is Jessica planning to use me to impress the representative from *Teenager Magazine*?" Brooke asked.

"Yes," Elizabeth told her. "Jessica's got this idea that if the family makes an effort, we can still win the trip to Paris."

"Do you think that's possible, Elizabeth?" Brooke asked doubtfully.

"No," Elizabeth replied. "Dad wanted Jessica to phone the magazine and drop out of the contest. But Mom said that we should play along with her, to teach her a lesson. If Jessica wants to exaggerate, we'll exaggerate, too." She giggled. "In fact, we've decided to be a model French family that no one will ever forget. If you want, you can help us."

Brooke grinned. "Sure. That'll be fun. If you want, I can give Jessica a few other suggestions, too. Like what the family should wear in

order to look more French. Of course, your outfits might be just a little on the weird side. But
we can tell Jessica that it's the latest from Paris.
Brookette ought to know what she's talking
about."

Elizabeth laughed. "That would be terrific,
Brooke! I'm sure Mom and Dad and Steve
would go along with that part of the joke, too."

"You know, Elizabeth," Brooke said, "I
think this Unicorn pledge task could turn out to
be really interesting after all."

"It'll probably be a lot more interesting than
Jessica expects it to be," Elizabeth agreed with
another laugh. "The Wakefields certainly aren't
going to win a trip to Paris. But we'll have a
great time losing!"

"Listen, everybody," Jessica announced
importantly that evening at dinner. "I've got
some wonderful news about Thursday night."

"Don't tell me," Mr. Wakefield said. "You've
decided to invite the French ambassador in
order to impress Ms. Harris."

Jessica smiled at her father's joke. "No, of
course not. But I *have* arranged for a French
maid to do the serving. She'll help Mom cook
the dinner, too."

Steven sputtered into his mashed potatoes,
and Mr. Wakefield stared at Jessica.

"A French maid?" Mrs. Wakefield asked,

feigning surprise. Earlier, Elizabeth had filled her in on Brooke's offer to go along with their plan. She didn't tell Mrs. Wakefield that it was also a Unicorn pledge task. She knew her mother didn't always approve of the things the Unicorns did.

Mr. Wakefield put down his fork. "Really, Jessica," he complained, "don't you think you're going a little too far with this thing?"

"Let's hear what Jessica has to say, Ned," Mrs. Wakefield said. "Who is this French maid?"

"And how much is she costing?" Mr. Wakefield added.

Jessica helped herself to some more mashed potatoes. "Actually, it's Brooke Dennis. She volunteered to do it as a favor. You know that Brooke spent a summer in Paris," Jessica went on smoothly. "She speaks French very well."

"So she can help us sprinkle a few French words into the conversation." Mrs. Wakefield nodded.

"That's right," Jessica said. "And she can help with the cooking. I'm sure she knows lots about French food."

"She probably knows a lot about French clothes, too," Elizabeth put in. "If we asked her, maybe she'd give us some tips on what to wear for a special French dinner like this one."

"Elizabeth, that's a great idea!" Jessica exclaimed enthusiastically. "We can dress up just like a French family."

"Dress up?" Steven asked with a frown. "You mean, I have to wear something formal?"

"Not formal," Elizabeth said quickly. "I'm sure Brooke will come up with some of the latest French fashions."

"That's right, Steven," Mrs. Wakefield said. "Wouldn't it be a good idea to know how the French boys dress? That way, you'll have some idea of what to pack for our trip to Paris."

Steven nodded. "Yeah, you're right, Mom," he agreed. "I'd hate to go to Paris looking like some hick from the sticks. Tell Brooke to come up with something for me to wear, will you, Elizabeth?" He grinned at at Jessica. "And you know what, Jess? I've figured out a way to impress Ms. Harris with my trombone playing. As soon as she hears me, she'll be ready to hand over our free tickets to Paris."

"I don't know, Steven," Jessica said doubtfully. "I hate to say it, but I'm afraid if she hears you play the trombone, she'll know I exaggerated."

"But that's the beauty of it," Steven exclaimed. "I'll tell her I'm going upstairs to practice, and then I'll put on a jazz trombone tape."

"Steven, that's wonderful!" Jessica exclaimed. "I'm sure a tape will make a terrific impression on her!"

"And I've decided on a clever way to handle all that stuff you wrote about my oil paintings," Mr. Wakefield said with a grin. "You can count on me, Jessica. I'm going to be the most interesting artist Ms. Harris has met in her entire life."

"Oh, Dad, thank you," Jessica breathed. It was just incredible the way everybody in her family was rallying around her. She turned to her mother. "Do you suppose we could have candles at the dinner?" she asked. "And maybe some flowers?"

"Elizabeth and I have been talking about dinner," Mrs. Wakefield said. "We've already come up with some ideas."

"I borrowed a French cookbook from the library this afternoon," Elizabeth said. "It's got a lot of neat stuff in it, Jessica. Like Braised Partridge Wings in Wine and Soufflé à la Terrapin."

Jessica looked at her sister doubtfully. "Soufflé à la Terrapin?" she asked. "Isn't a Terrapin a kind of turtle? I think they're on the endangered species list."

"Well, maybe Soufflé à la Terrapin isn't exactly the right dish," Elizabeth said. "But there are lots of other dishes. *Escargots*, for instance."

"What's that?" Steven asked suspiciously.

"Snails," Elizabeth replied.

Steven shook his head. "Forget it," he said. "I couldn't eat one of those, even if it meant winning a *year* in Paris."

Elizabeth smiled. "Well, I guess the *escargots* are out. But wait until you hear what we're having for dessert!"

Steven looked doubtful. "What is it?"

"A *flambé*," Mrs. Wakefield said triumphantly.

Mr. Wakefield grinned at Steven. "You'll like it, Steven. It's very dramatic. The chef pours brandy over your dessert. Then he lights it with a match and it catches on fire."

Mrs. Wakefield beamed. "A *flambé* is terribly spectacular and extremely chic. They serve it in all the finest French restaurants."

Elizabeth leaned forward. "Mom and I will do all we can to make sure that Ms. Harris has an interesting meal, Jessica. One that she'll never forget."

"This is great!" Jessica cried. "I can't believe I was actually dreading this interview!"

Steven grinned at her. "Just wait. You haven't seen anything yet."

"Steven's right," Mr. Wakefield said. "The best is yet to come."

Jessica broke into an ecstatic smile. Maybe she had exaggerated a few of the details when she had filled out her contest entry form, but that didn't matter. Her family *was* a model family. They were as close to perfect as any family could possibly be.

Eight

◇

Jessica was so excited about the way things were going that she could hardly wait for school to be over on Wednesday.

"Ellen and I are going shopping at the mall," Lila told her as they walked to their lockers after class. "Want to come? My father gave me some money to spend, and I'm thinking of getting something new to wear to the Dynamo concert next week."

For once, Jessica didn't mind Lila's bragging. "Thanks for the invitation," she said. "But I've got something important to do this afternoon, and I have to rush right home and get started."

"I suppose this has to do with that stupid contest," Lila said scornfully.

Jessica lifted her chin. "Yes, it does."

Lila shook her head. "I just don't understand why you're wasting time with it, Jessica. You're going to do a lot of work for nothing."

"Who knows?" Jessica tried to keep her voice light, but inside, she was beginning to fume.

"Maybe I should have entered the contest," Lila said thoughtfully. "After all, my father speaks fluent French, and we have a French gardener. I'll bet we would have won."

By now, Jessica was furious. Lila went on talking, unaware of her friend's mood.

"I'm sorry you won't come shopping," Lila said complacently. "I know just what I'm going to buy. I saw a unicorn ring that exactly matches the unicorn earrings I got a few weeks ago."

Jessica gritted her teeth. "Well, have a good time," she said as she turned away. *The nerve of Lila*, she thought, *being so sure that she could win the contest!* But Jessica didn't have time to be angry. She had something else to do that would require all her energy.

With Ms. Harris coming for dinner tomorrow night, Jessica wanted the house to be absolutely spotless. When she got home she put on her oldest clothes and then rummaged through the kitchen. She pulled out all the cleaning supplies she could find, including brooms and mops and dustcloths and waxes and sprays.

Then she began an intensive clean-up. In the living room, she dusted the furniture, vacuumed the carpet, and washed the windows. She polished the dining room table and chairs, and cleaned the mirror over the buffet.

Jessica was straightening the magazines on the coffee table in the den when her mother got home from work. "Jessica?" Mrs. Wakefield asked, glancing around the den incredulously. "Did *you* do all this?"

"I came straight home from school," Jessica said, looking around proudly. "I've been working for the past hour. The living room, the dining room—"

"Jessica," Mrs. Wakefield said carefully, "you're not in any trouble at school, are you? Is this report card week?"

Jessica laughed. "Of course I'm not in any trouble. And report cards don't come out for another couple of weeks. I just want our house to look good for Ms. Harris, that's all."

"Well, I must say, this room has never looked better," Mrs. Wakefield said admiringly. "If the other rooms look as good, Ms. Harris will think that our model family lives in a model house."

"I'm going to do the downstairs bathroom next," Jessica said. "And then the bedrooms. I thought I'd scrub the kitchen floor, too."

Mrs. Wakefield smiled. "Maybe we ought

to encourage you to enter more contests, Jessica."

Jessica thought seriously about her mother's suggestion for a moment. It had been fun to dream up wonderful things about her family. But there was a lot more work and worry involved with the contest than she could ever have imagined. She shook her head. "I think one contest is enough for a while."

Mrs. Wakefield laughed. "It's enough for me, too."

By the time dinner was ready, Jessica had finished cleaning all of the downstairs rooms. She was so tired she was ready to drop. She ate absentmindedly, thinking about all the other things she still had to do. When dinner was over, she pushed back her plate and put her elbows on the table.

"I'm just about ready to collapse," she said wearily. "House-cleaning is a lot more tiring than I thought." She looked around the table. "Please, everybody, keep the house clean until after tomorrow night."

"Don't forget that it's your turn to do the dishes this evening, Jessica," Mrs. Wakefield reminded her.

"Elizabeth," Jessica said plaintively, "can we trade? I'm so exhausted, I don't think I could lift even one dish. And I've still got a lot of cleaning to do upstairs."

Steven grinned. "You didn't have much trouble lifting the dishes a few minutes ago, Jessica. I saw you take thirds on the casserole."

Jessica was too tired to do anything more than stick out her tongue at Steven.

"All right," Elizabeth said comfortingly. "I'll help you with the dishes, Jessica. Anyway, we want to get finished quickly. Brooke is coming over this evening."

"She is?" Jessica said, suddenly feeling not quite so tired. "Do you think she would give me a French lesson? I'd like to know just a few words and phrases, like 'my name is Jessica' and 'how are you.' Easy stuff like that."

Elizabeth smiled. "I'm sure she can help. Actually, though, she's coming to give us advice about our outfits. I told her that we wanted to look really French for Ms. Harris."

"Do you suppose she could tell me what a French artist is likely to wear?" Mr. Wakefield asked.

"I'm not sure that you should get dressed up like an artist, Dad," Jessica said doubtfully. "We don't want to lay it on too thick. Ms. Harris might suspect something."

"I don't think Ms. Harris is going to suspect anything, Jessica," Mrs. Wakefield put in quickly.

Elizabeth smothered a giggle and Jessica looked at her curiously.

Mr. Wakefield pushed back his chair. "I'll be in my workshop if Brooke has any ideas for me." He grinned at Jessica. "A famous painter has to spend a little time painting, you know."

Jessica forgot about Elizabeth's giggle and smiled at her father. "Thanks for being such a good sport, Dad."

"Just wait until tomorrow night," Mr. Wakefield said with a grin. "You'll see what a terrific sport I am."

"Come on, Jessica," Elizabeth said cheerfully. "I'll get these dishes done while you finish cleaning upstairs."

The kitchen chores were finished by the time Brooke arrived. Elizabeth hurried to the door to let her in. Brooke was carrying a suitcase in one hand and she had a box tucked under her other arm.

"Did you find any costumes?" Elizabeth asked in a low voice, taking the box from Brooke.

"I found a bunch of good stuff in an old trunk of my father's," Brooke whispered back. "I don't know if it looks very French, but it certainly looks weird."

Elizabeth giggled. "The weirder the better, as long as Jessica thinks it's French. Mom said she could probably come up with something too. She's got a bunch of scarves and jewelry and things."

"Hi, Brooke," Jessica called from the top of the stairs. "What are you two whispering about?"

"I was telling Brooke that you wanted her to give you a French lesson," Elizabeth said. "Just a few simple words."

"I'd be glad to give you a lesson," Brooke told Jessica. "French isn't hard to learn, really."

Jessica smiled. "Come on upstairs, Brooke. Let's see what you've brought!"

As they went into Jessica's bedroom, Elizabeth looked around in surprise. "Wow, Jess," she said. "I've never seen your room look so neat!"

"I thought we'd show Ms. Harris around the house," Jessica explained. She turned to Brooke. "Ms. Harris is the woman from the magazine. She's the guest I mentioned to you. It's really important to impress her. She's got a lot of say on who wins the trip to Paris."

"Elizabeth told me all about Ms. Harris and what you're trying to do," Brooke said. "I'm glad you thought of putting my pledge task together with your dinner, Jessica."

"Lending us these clothes will help us a lot," Elizabeth put in. "Let's see what you've brought."

Brooke put the suitcase on the bed. "Here we are," she announced, unzipping it. "The latest in ultra-French style!"

Eagerly, Jessica rummaged through the clothes. She pulled out a long swirly skirt made of a wrinkled, gauzy-looking fabric in shades of orange and magenta. "This is in fashion in Paris?" she asked doubtfully, holding it up to her waist. The skirt came down almost to her ankles.

"Certainment!" Brooke exclaimed. She kissed her fingertips in an exaggerated French gesture. "Eet is zee latest fashion."

Jessica wrinkled her nose. "It looks like it came out of some old trunk."

"It looks very French to me," Elizabeth said, trying not to smile. She pulled out a magenta-colored tee-shirt. "Is this the sort of thing Jessica should wear with the skirt, Brooke?"

"Me?" Jessica asked worriedly, looking at the floppy tee-shirt and the gauzy skirt. "You think I ought to wear this? Don't the colors sort of, well, clash?"

"But clashing colors are the latest fashion statement in Paris," Brooke assured her. "This is exactly the kind of outfit you'd wear to go to Montmartre. That's the famous Bohemian district of Paris, where everybody goes to see shows and art galleries and to have fun."

Mrs. Wakefield came into the room. "Hello, Brooke," she said. "Have you brought us some clothes to wear to our French dinner?"

"What do you think of this, Mom?" Jessica

asked uncertainly, holding up the skirt and tee-shirt.

"That's what Brooke is suggesting for Jessica," Elizabeth put in. "Isn't it terrific?"

"Ooh la la!" Mrs. Wakefield cried. "Jessica, that outfit is *perfect* for you!"

"It is?" Jessica asked.

"Perfectly Parisian," her mother said. "And I think I have just the jewelry to go with it. Remember the green plastic necklace and bracelets that Steven gave me a couple of years ago?"

Elizabeth smiled. She knew that her mother tried to like everything her children bought for her. But she couldn't remember ever seeing her mother wear the green plastic jewelry set.

"But that jewelry was hideous. Anyway, this blouse is magenta. Won't green look a little weird?"

"Green!" Brooke cried, clasping her hands ecstatically. "What a marvelous idea! Green is exactly the right French accent, Mrs. Wakefield! *Perfectement!"*

"Well, if you say so," Jessica replied with a sigh. "What kind of shoes should I wear?"

"Your ballet slippers would be fine," Brooke said, "tied up high around your ankles." She fished through the box. "And here's a pair of red tights. They go with the skirt."

"Yuch," Jessica said, closing her eyes. "Red tights, green jewelry, a magenta top—"

"Of course," Elizabeth said, "if you don't want to be fashionable, you don't have to—"

Jessica's eyes popped open and she clutched the red tights. "Of course I want to be fashionable. It's just that I get a little queasy when I think of the color combination."

"You know what they say in Paris," Brooke said.

"What do they say in Paris?' Mrs. Wakefield wanted to know.

"The wilder the better," Brooke said firmly. "The Parisians love the Bohemian look."

"What did you bring for Elizabeth?" Jessica asked.

Elizabeth plunged her arms into the suitcase and came up with a pair of purple jeans with double rows of rhinestones down the sides. "How about these, Brooke?"

"That's exactly what I had in mind for you, Elizabeth." Brooke reached into the box. "You could wear them with this black top. A pair of black boots would look really cute."

Jessica grimaced. "Those rhinestones are utterly gross, Elizabeth."

"But that's because we don't know the French styles, Jess," Elizabeth said. "As long as Brooke says it looks Parisian, that's all I care about."

"I know what would look nice with that outfit," Mrs. Wakefield said. "I've got a long purple scarf. You could wind it around your neck several times. That's a very Continental look."

"And with the scarf," Brooke added, "you should wear this!" With a flourish, she pulled out a little black felt hat.

"Terrific!" Elizabeth clapped the hat on her head. "Brooke, what do you suggest for Mom?"

"I've already decided what I'm going to wear," Mrs. Wakefield said. "I looked through a French magazine today. I'm going to wear a denim skirt over my leotard, and a pair of red leg warmers." She glanced at Jessica. "You see, Brooke, Jessica told Ms. Harris about my love of dance."

"Leg warmers!" Brooke exclaimed. "The perfect touch! I hope you'll wear lots of jewelry, too. The French *love* jewelry. The more the better."

Mrs. Wakefield snapped her fingers. "I know!" she said. "I'll wear my silver Eiffel Tower earrings!"

"Oh, Mom, not those tacky things!" Jessica groaned. "They're horrible. I only bought you those as a joke! They hang down to your shoulders."

"But they're perfect for my outfit," Mrs. Wakefield said. "Don't you think so, Brooke?"

"*Absolument*," Brooke said. "Dangly earrings are really in style, Jessica. When you get to Paris, you'll see earrings dangling all over the place."

Elizabeth could hardly keep from laughing. "Then it looks like we're all set," she said. "But what about Steven?"

Brooke pulled a black turtleneck sweater and a black leather vest out of her box. The vest was studded with pieces of silver-colored metal. "This is for Steven," she said. "If he has a pair of black jeans, they'd be perfect."

"Black leather?" Jessica asked doubtfully.

"Of course," Elizabeth said. "Haven't you seen outfits like this on MTV?"

"Sure, but that's television," Jessica said. "I mean, those are musicians. They're supposed to look weird."

"But Steven plays the trombone," Mrs. Wakefield pointed out.

"With this outfit, Steven will really look like a jazz musician," Elizabeth added.

"I guess," Jessica agreed finally. "But all of this looks kind of strange to me. I don't know if Ms. Harris—"

"If she has any doubt about whether you are a French-oriented family," Brooke said firmly, "these outfits will clinch it."

"I agree with Brooke," Mrs. Wakefield said. "To our American eyes, these clothes might look a little strange. But when we're in Paris—"

She turned to Jessica. "You still want to go to Paris, don't you, Jessica?"

Jessica nodded. In the beginning, she'd thought that they didn't have a chance. But now that they were finalists, it seemed that they had as good a chance as anybody. *Why not make every effort?* she asked herself. It would be worth all the effort just to see Lila's face when she announced that she and her family were going to Paris!

"Well, fine, then," Mrs. Wakefield said. She picked up the leather vest. "I'll take this to Steven."

"Are you ready to begin your French lesson, Jessica?" Brooke asked.

"Yes," Jessica said.

"That's *oui*," Brooke said. *"Oui* means *yes."*

"Oui," Jessica pronounced carefully, shaping her lips just the way Brooke did. *"Oui."*

"Bien," Brooke said, with an approving smile. "That means *good. Très bien* means *very good."*

"Oui," Jessica said happily. *"Très bien."*

Nine

◇

It was almost six-thirty on Thursday evening, and Elizabeth was in the kitchen helping her mother get ready for the dinner. Earlier, she had gotten dressed in her "French" outfit. She had pulled her hair to one side and braided it, then fastened the braid into a loop over her ear.

The doorbell rang and Elizabeth went to open it. Brooke was standing outside in her raincoat. Underneath it, she wore a French maid's black uniform, with a ruffled apron and a little white cap.

Elizabeth giggled. "Brooke, you look terrific, just like a genuine French maid. Wait until Jessica sees you."

"And you, *ma chère*," Brooke said with a

grin. "I love your hair pulled over to one side that way. And those jeans, they are so *chic!*"

Elizabeth laughed, looking down at her rhinestone-trimmed jeans. "Oh, these old things?" she asked. "I think they came out of somebody's trunk."

Mrs. Wakefield turned around as the girls came into the kitchen. "What do you think of my outfit, Brooke?"

Brooke nodded approvingly. "You look as if you just left the ballet studio, Mrs. Wakefield."

Mrs. Wakefield looked at her leg warmers and ballet slippers. "I'm not overdoing it?" she asked.

Elizabeth shook her head. "No, Mom, you look cute. Especially with those Eiffel Tower earrings. They're the perfect touch."

Mrs. Wakefield tossed her head so that her earrings caught the light. "They are rather outrageous, aren't they? What do you suppose Ms. Harris will make of them, and of the rest of our outfits?"

Brooke smiled. "She'll probably think this is the wackiest family she's ever met." She glanced toward the stove. "What did you finally decide on for tonight's menu?"

Mrs. Wakefield picked up a spoon. "For the main course, we're having a famous French specialty. At least, it'll soon be famous. It was Elizabeth's idea, so we've given her name to it."

"What is it, Elizabeth?" Brooke asked.

"It's called *Nouilles au fromage à la Elizabeth*," Elizabeth said.

Brooke frowned. "But that translates to—"

"Right!" Elizabeth grinned wickedly. "Good old American macaroni and cheese! It's one of Jessica's favorite dishes."

Brooke giggled. "What did Jessica say when you told her what you're serving?"

"We told her the French name," Elizabeth said. "I guess she's still trying to figure out what it means. Anyway, she has strict orders to stay out of the kitchen. She's upstairs right now getting ready for the big night."

"Well, I'm all finished," Steven announced, coming into the kitchen. "Whew! That was hard work!"

"Thanks for helping out," Mrs. Wakefield said. "Did you do every room?"

Steven took an apple off the table and polished it on his sleeve. "Yeah," he said. "Every room. And I did a great job, too. I really messed things up." He shook his head and grinned. "This is the first time in my life that you ever told me to make a *mess*, Mom.

"It's probably the last time, too," Elizabeth said with a laugh.

"A dirty house is part of the plan?" Brooke asked.

Elizabeth nodded. "Mom, where are the candles?"

Steven grinned. "Candles are part of the plan too," he told Brooke.

Upstairs, Jessica was trying to decide which was the front and which was the back of her floppy magenta tee-shirt. Then, deciding that it probably didn't matter, she pulled it on over her head. Finally, she added her mother's green necklace.

Yuch, she thought, staring at herself in the mirror. *What a combination. Those French certainly have a strange sense of color.*

Jessica put on the green bracelets, and then tied her ballet slippers, crossing the strings high up on her ankles. She thought excitedly of the evening ahead. It was going to be terrific. She smiled, imagining the wonderful French dish her mother and Elizabeth were cooking right now in the kitchen. *Nouilles au fromage à la Elizabeth*, that's what they'd called it. She didn't know what the words meant, but it sounded terribly French and very sophisticated. She was sure it was going to taste fabulous.

At that moment, the doorbell rang. Jessica paused, expecting somebody to answer it. Nobody did. After a few seconds, Jessica hurried downstairs. On her way down, she nearly stumbled over a stack of old newspapers. She noticed Steven's sweater dangling on a chair in the hallway, and her father's golf bag leaning against the closet door.

But Jessica didn't have time to wonder why the hallway was so cluttered. The doorbell was still ringing, and she hurried to open the door. A woman with her black hair in a French braid was standing on the step, holding an umbrella.

"Hello," the woman said pleasantly. "My name is Ms. Harris. I've come to interview the Wakefields for the *Teenager Magazine* contest."

"*Bonjour*, Mademoiselle Harris," Jessica said. "*Je m'appelle Jessica. Comment allez-vous?*" Last night she had practiced the French for "My name is Jessica" and "How are you?" at least a hundred times. Now she spoke slowly and very carefully, hoping she was getting it right.

The woman broke into a smile. "Ah, *oui*, Jessica," she said, "*Je vais bien, merci*," which Jessica knew meant "I'm well, thank you." Then she went on in a stream of rapid French that was completely incomprehensible to Jessica.

Jessica's eyes widened. She had used up half of her French on that one short sentence. What was she supposed to say next? Brooke had taught her a little phrase about the weather being nice. "*Il fait beau*," she said.

Ms. Harris looked at Jessica with a puzzled expression as she shook out her umbrella. "But

I'm afraid the weather's *not* very beautiful. It's been raining all day."

Jessica blushed. "You're right," she said, looking up at the sky. "I hadn't noticed." She opened the door wider. "Ah, won't you come in, Ms. Harris?"

Jessica took Ms. Harris's jacket, moving the golf bag out of the way so that she could open the closet door. Unfortunately, the golf bag fell over and hit Ms. Harris on the foot. Ms. Harris jumped back and said a few words in French. From her tone, Jessica knew that she was asking a question, but she didn't have a clue as to what Ms. Harris was saying.

Jessica shifted uneasily from one foot to the other. They were going to have to stop speaking French, or she'd never know what was going on. "Excuse me," she said, feeling flustered, "I didn't quite understand. Would you mind saying that again?"

Ms. Harris looked at her. "I asked you," she said in English, "whether your father plays golf."

"Oh, yes, I mean, *oui*, he does." Jessica shoved the golf bag into the closet, her face flaming. "He's an excellent golfer. Of course," she added hurriedly, "he doesn't have much time to play. He spends most of his time painting."

Jessica led the way into the living room she

had cleaned so carefully the day before. What she saw made her gasp. The floor was littered with newspapers, the sofa cushions were topsy-turvy, the lamp shades were crooked. It looked as though there had been a wild party in the room.

"Ah, excuse me a moment," Jessica muttered, straightening the sofa cushions. She picked up a few of the newspapers. "I guess my brother and some of his friends must have been here," she said, trying to come up with a plausible explanation for the mess.

Mrs. Harris laughed. "Maybe he and his trombone ensemble were practicing," she said, as she sat down on the sofa. There was a loud, startling *pop!* and she jumped up again with a little yelp.

"Excuse me," Jessica said. She picked up the sofa cushion. Underneath it there was a burst balloon. "It must have been left from . . . from our last party."

Looking slightly bemused, Ms. Harris sat down again. "I must say," she began, "that the judges were very impressed with your contest entry, Jessica. You seem to have a very unique family."

Jessica cast her eyes down. "I think so, too." She wondered which one of her unique family had messed up the room.

"I've been looking forward to this interview," Ms. Harris continued, reaching into her bag. She pulled out a notebook and flipped the pages. "I've made some notes on the questions I want to ask you. Shall we begin?"

But before they could start, Elizabeth came dashing in. "Oh, *ma belle soeur!*" she exclaimed when she saw Jessica. She ran to her and kissed her on both cheeks.

Jessica was taken aback. That wasn't planned. "Ah, Mademoiselle Harris," she said, "*Permettez-moi de vous présenter ma soeur Elizabeth.*" She had now used up all of her French in introducing Ms. Harris to Elizabeth. Now she'd either have to repeat herself or speak in English.

"*E-leez-ee-bet,*" Elizabeth corrected Jessica in an exaggerated French accent. "My name is Eleezeebet."

"I'm glad to meet you, *Eleezeebet,*" Ms. Harris said with a smile. "Jessica wrote wonderful things about you in her essay."

Elizabeth put her arm around Jessica's shoulder. "Jessica is really the wonderful one," she gushed. "And she's always wanted to go to Paris. It's been the dream of her life."

Jessica looked at Elizabeth, horrified by her sister's behavior. Why was she dropping hints like that? What was she trying to do? Wreck everything?

But Ms. Harris didn't seem to notice anything out of the ordinary. "I think that Paris is the one city in the world that everybody wants to visit," she said. She looked at Jessica. "But you'd have to brush up on your French a little," she said with a smile. "By the way, how many French classes have you taken?"

"We haven't taken any, actually," Jessica confessed. "At our school, we don't take languages until seventh grade. But as I said in my essay," she added hurriedly, "we *do* speak it at home. Some of the time, anyway."

Brooke stepped into the room, wearing her French maid's uniform. *"Le dinêr est prêt, mesdemoiselles,"* she announced loudly.

It was the moment Jessica had been waiting for. Ms. Harris would certainly be impressed. "Allow me to present Brookette," she said proudly. "She's our French maid."

"Brookette" dropped a modest little curtsey and Ms. Harris raised her eyebrows. "You didn't mention Brookette in your contest entry, Jessica."

Jessica hadn't thought of that. "Brookette has just arrived," she explained lamely. "From Paris."

"I see," Ms. Harris replied.

The three of them followed Brooke into the dining room. Jessica looked at the table with relief. At least the table was set very nicely, complete with flowers and candles.

Then Mr. Wakefield came into the dining

room. To Jessica's surprise, her father was wearing an artist's smock liberally stained with paint. A beret sat on his head at a smart angle and an artist's brush was stuck behind his ear like a pencil.

"Bonjour," he said.

"You must be Mr. Wakefield," Ms. Harris said with a smile.

Mr. Wakefield bowed low over her hand. "We are honored to have you with us this evening, Mademoiselle Harris," he said. "Please sit down."

Jessica sat down too. She had hoped that her father would go along with her story that he was a painter, but she hadn't imagined that he would go *this* far! His conversation seemed to be pretty normal, though. If only he would take off his beret and remove the brush from behind his ear! She'd never dreamed that her father could be so impolite.

Jessica was distracted by Steven's entrance. If she had been upset when she saw how her father was dressed, she was even more upset when she saw her brother. He was wearing black jeans and the black sweater and vest that Brooke had loaned him. That was bad enough, but his hair looked even worse. It was slicked back on the sides and pulled up to a sharp point on the top of his head. Jessica felt mortified.

Since when, she wondered, *did Steven become a punk?*

"*Bonjour*," Steven muttered, scraping his chair on the floor. He slumped into the seat and put both elbows on the table.

"This is our son, Steven." Mr. Wakefield beamed at Steven. "We are very proud of him. He's on his way to becoming a big musician."

"I understand that you play the trombone, Steven," Ms. Harris said pleasantly.

Steven grunted.

"You'll have to forgive him," Mr. Wakefield apologized. "All musicians are temperamental, you know. Sometimes he acts a little strangely, but we make allowances."

Jessica gulped. What was her family trying to do to her? And then her mother came into the room. She was wearing an enormous white apron and a tall chef's cap. She looked like something straight out of a comic strip.

"Hi!" Mrs. Wakefield said breezily. "I'm Alice Wakefield." She tossed her cap into the corner and pulled off her apron. "Hope you don't mind if I wear my leotard to dinner," she added, as she sat down at the table. "I just got home from the dance studio. But I still had time to whip up a gourmet French dinner."

Ms. Harris nodded. "I see."

"Shall we get cozy?" Mrs. Wakefield reached up and turned off the light switch. The room darkened, and the three candles on the table flickered.

"Hey!" Steven exclaimed. "It's dark in here! How am I going to see what I'm eating?"

"I'm sure you'll think of a way to manage, son," Mr. Wakefield said mildly.

Steven got up, went to the buffet, and pulled a flashlight out of a drawer. "There," he said, turning the flashlight on and directing it at his plate. "OK," he announced. "I'm ready to eat."

"Wait until you hear what we're having for dinner," Jessica said hurriedly to Ms. Harris. "It's *Nouilles au fromage à la Elizabeth*. It's named after my sister," she added. "Elizabeth invented it."

Ms. Harris smiled. "The dish has an intriguing name," she said. "I'm anxious to taste it."

"Well, then, let's get started," Mrs. Wakefield said. She clapped her hands dramatically. "Brookette! Please serve our dinner."

Brookette came through the door, bearing the elaborate silver dish that the Wakefields only used at Christmas and on other holidays. When Brookette put the dish on the table, Jessica leaned forward eagerly, trying to see in the dim candlelight. Steven grabbed the dish and pulled it toward him. He heaped his plate full and began to shovel the food into his mouth.

"Macaroni and cheese!" Jessica exclaimed before she could stop herself. She loved macaroni and cheese, but it certainly wasn't an exotic French dish!

"*Nouilles au fromage*," Ms. Harris murmured. "An American dish dressed up with a French name. How clever."

"And we're having two other favorites," Mrs. Wakefield said enthusiastically, as Brooke brought in two more dishes. "*Épinards à la crème* and *Pain de carottes*."

"What's that?" Steven asked suspiciously.

"Creamed spinach and carrot loaf," Elizabeth told him.

Steven made a gagging sound.

Mr. Wakefield leaned forward. "Even musicians have to eat their vegetables, dear boy," he said gently.

Steven finished the last of his macaroni and cheese and pushed his chair back. "Not me," he said loudly, wiping his mouth with the back of his hand. "*Pain de carottes* is a pain! I'm going upstairs to practice my trombone. A little dinner music."

"That will be lovely," Ms. Harris said with a smile.

"But you'll miss dessert, *mon cher*," Mrs. Wakefield protested.

Steven stopped in the doorway. "What is it?"

Elizabeth nudged Jessica. "You tell everyone what we're having, Jess," she said in a loud whisper.

Jessica squirmed nervously. She had no idea what had been going on for the last few minutes, or why her family was doing this to her. Ms. Harris turned to her expectantly.

"We, uh, we're having a *flambé*," Jessica said. "They have it in all the best French restaurants, you know!" She couldn't resist the temptation of adding, "My mother always makes the most gourmet desserts."

"*Bon!*" Ms. Harris exclaimed. "What kind of a *flambé* are we having? *Crêpe suzettes flambé?*"

Mrs. Wakefield smiled triumphantly. "*Jelly doughnuts flambé.*"

Mr. Wakefield clapped. "My favorite!" he cried. "Are they raspberry?"

"*Oui, mon cher,*" Mrs. Wakefield said, beaming. "I wouldn't buy any other kind."

Jessica felt like crawling under the table. She couldn't imagine why Ms. Harris just smiled and nodded and kept on eating her creamed spinach as if nothing were wrong. She must just be too polite to say anything.

A few minutes later, as if things weren't already bad enough, Steven's concert began. It started off well enough, and Jessica relaxed a little when the first notes of the jazz tape began to play.

But a moment later, Steven turned the tape off and began to practice for real. The noise was horrible. Jessica cringed. She knew she had exaggerated Steven's talent, but she couldn't remember that he had ever been *this* bad. The family's conversation could barely be heard over the racket, and by the time dinner was over, they were all shouting at one another.

"That was an excellent dinner, Mrs. Wakefield," Ms. Harris shouted.

"Thank you," Mrs. Wakefield shouted back.

"I'd like you to see my studio," Mr. Wakefield yelled. "And my latest painting project."

"That would be nice," Ms. Harris yelled back, at the top of her lungs.

At that moment, Brooke came in to clear the table. "Brookette," Mrs. Wakefield said, "perhaps you'd like to visit Mr. Wakefield's studio with us."

"*Oui, madame*," Brooke said.

On the way to Mr. Wakefield's workshop, they were joined by Steven.

"What a lovely concert, Steven," Mrs. Wakefield told him warmly.

By this time, Jessica was so humiliated that all she wanted to do was go upstairs and crawl into her bed. But she couldn't. She had to go along with the others.

An easel covered with a cloth was set up

in the middle of the workshop. With a flourish, Mr. Wakefield pulled back the cloth.

"*Voilà*," he said proudly.

Jessica stared. The canvas was a muddy-looking mess of splotches and runny patches. It was the worst piece of art Jessica had ever seen.

"It's a copy of a Manet," Mr. Wakefield told Ms. Harris.

Ms. Harris nodded politely. "Of course."

"*Très bon*," Brooke said, sounding very impressed.

"Dad, that's very nice," Elizabeth added. "That's one of your very best paintings."

Jessica blinked. How could everybody say such wonderful things about such a horrible painting?

"And now *I* have a surprise," Mrs. Wakefield said happily. "I'm going to perform a short ballet dance in the den. Jessica and Elizabeth, would you take Ms. Harris on a tour of the house while I get into my costume?"

Jessica stared at her mother. Perform a short dance? But her mother didn't dance ballet! Take a tour of the house? But what if the rest of it was as messy as the living room? Suddenly, she had had all she could take.

"No!" she cried.

For a second or two, there was silence.

"Jessica," Mr. Wakefield said finally, "is

something wrong?" The corners of his mouth began to twitch.

Beside Jessica, Elizabeth and Brooke giggled. Steven chuckled, and Mrs. Wakefield began to laugh.

Jessica turned to look at the magazine representative. Even Ms. Harris was wearing a broad smile!

"What's wrong?" Jessica repeated, as everybody laughed. "Will someone please tell me what's going on here?"

Ten

◇

When Ms. Harris finally caught her breath, she turned to Jessica. "I think," she said gently, "that your family arranged a little joke tonight."

"A joke?" Jessica asked.

"We apologize for playing this trick on you, Jessica," Mrs. Wakefield said, still smiling. "But we did it to teach you a lesson about exaggeration."

"That's right," Mr. Wakefield said. He pulled off his painter's smock.

Ms. Harris looked at Jessica. "Your mother called me and gave me an idea of what had happened. But I think it would be helpful if you filled me in on the details, Jessica."

Jessica looked at the floor. She could feel

her face turning red. "I . . . I entered the contest accidently," she confessed.

Ms. Harris raised her eyebrows. "Accidently?" she asked. "How in the world can anybody enter a contest accidently?"

Jessica told Ms. Harris how she had written the essay for fun, without intending to send it in, how it had gotten in the mail by mistake, and how she had tried to talk her family into pretending that they were French-oriented. As she talked, she realized how ridiculous the story sounded. The longer she talked, the worse she felt.

"I know that I should have called the magazine and told the truth," she said miserably. "I've wasted your time and maybe even kept another family from being finalists. It was dumb to think that we could win the trip to Paris."

"Did you read the contest rules before you filled out the application?" Ms. Harris asked.

"No," Jessica replied. "The print was too fine. Why?"

"Because if you had," Ms. Harris said, "you would have realized that you have to be enrolled in a French class at school in order to qualify for the contest. So even if your family had won first prize, Jessica, you wouldn't have been able to accept it."

"Oh." Jessica felt completely humiliated.

Ms. Harris laughed kindly. "Don't be too

hard on yourself, Jessica," she said. "You do have a pretty terrific family, with a great sense of humor. I agree that it wasn't right for you to exaggerate. And you *must* learn to read the rules before you enter another contest. But the contest is an annual affair. You can enter again next year, when you are taking French."

"If you couldn't see the fine print, Jessica," Mrs. Wakefield said, "perhaps you ought to have your eyes checked. I wouldn't want you to make another mistake like this."

Jessica looked at her mother in horror. *Glasses!* she thought, alarmed. She couldn't imagine anything as horrible as having to wear glasses. "Oh, no, Mom," she said hurriedly. "I'm sure my eyes are just fine."

Ms. Harris looked around at everyone and smiled. "I really have to be going now," she said. "Thank you all for providing me with such an interesting evening. I don't know when I have been more entertained." Her smile broadened. "And I must confess that I've never seen such spectacular flaming doughnuts."

"And thank *you*," Mr. Wakefield said, grinning, "for being such a good sport."

They all went upstairs. Ms. Harris shook hands with everybody. Then she turned to Jessica. "Jessica, there's a consolation prize for each finalist. I'll be sending it to you very soon."

"A prize!" Jessica exclaimed, perking up a little. "That's wonderful."

"*Au revoir*," Ms. Harris said.

"*Au revoir*," everyone echoed.

After the door had closed behind Ms. Harris, Jessica took a deep breath and looked around at her family and Brooke. "I'm really sorry about all this," she said contritely. "I never really meant to enter the contest. But I was so fed up with Lila's bragging. I mean, I've got a terrific family, and I wanted to brag about you guys." She hung her head. "I guess I got carried away. But I'll never exaggerate again."

Steven hooted. "I'll believe that when I see it!"

Mrs. Wakefield put her arm around Jessica's shoulders. "Well, it all turned out fine," she said. "We had fun being outrageously French for the evening. And Ms. Harris *was* a good sport."

Jessica nodded. It had been a traumatic evening, but now it was over. Suddenly, a horrible thought occurred to her. Lila and Ellen had planned to drop by sometime during the evening. What if they'd changed their minds and had decided to peek in the window, after all? What if they had seen the Wakefields dressed in their strange outfits and acting so odd? Jessica moaned. If Lila knew what had gone on tonight, Jessica would never be able to live it down. She might as well resign as a Unicorn. She would be humiliated forever.

Jessica woke up the next morning with a terrible feeling of dread. The thought of facing Lila was like a heavy weight on her shoulders. Even though Brooke had promised not to tell what had really happened, there was always the possibility that Lila had seen it all.

Unfortunately, Lila was the first person Jessica saw when she got to homeroom that morning.

"Well?" Lila demanded. "How did Brooke do with her pledge task?"

Jessica's heart beat faster. "You mean, you didn't see?"

Lila shook her head. "Ellen and I were just ready to leave for your house when my father came home. He absolutely insisted on treating us to a French dinner at Chez Sam's. So we didn't make it to your house. How did Brooke do?"

Jessica felt a hundred times better. "Brooke did a great job," she said enthusiastically. "She wore her uniform and served dinner and spoke French. She did all the things we asked her to do." She smiled at Lila. "The dinner was a total success. In fact, the magazine representative said that she didn't know when she had been more entertained."

Lila harumphed. "I still don't think you're going to win the contest."

"Probably not," Jessica agreed with a shrug. "But I'm getting a big consolation prize."

Lila looked skeptical. "A prize?" Then she laughed. "Well, if you're lucky, it'll turn out to be a free dinner at Chez Sam's. We had such an incredible meal there last night." She paused. "By the way, what did you serve at your dinner?"

Jessica lifted her chin. "My mother cooked her famous French specialty. *Nouilles au fromage.* And for dessert, we had a spectacular *flambé.* Ms. Harris said she'd never seen anything like it."

To Jessica's satisfaction, Lila actually seemed impressed.

The next Monday, Elizabeth and Brooke were standing in front of Elizabeth's locker when Lila and Ellen came up to them.

"I'm glad to announce, Brooke," Lila said, "that this weekend the Unicorns voted unanimously to let you into the club. Congratulations."

Elizabeth looked at Brooke. What would she do?

"Thank you," Brooke said politely. "But I've decided I don't want to be a Unicorn."

Ellen's mouth fell open. "But why did you

do the pledge task if you didn't want to be a Unicorn?" she asked in surprise.

"Because I thought it would be fun." Brooke grinned at Elizabeth. "And because Jessica and Elizabeth needed me to help them out with their dinner."

"But . . . but I thought you were dying to get in," Lila said, dumbfounded. "What am I going to tell the Unicorns?"

Brooke looked at her. "You might tell them I'm allergic to purple," she suggested helpfully.

Elizabeth burst out laughing while Lila and Ellen walked away, speechless.

But Jessica didn't have much to laugh about during the week. As the Friday night Dynamo concert grew near, it was harder and harder for her to be around Lila. Jessica couldn't stand hearing about Lila's sky box seat. To make it even more unbearable, the seats that she and Elizabeth and Steven had gotten for the concert were terrible. They were all the way in the back, and far over to one side.

"Those seats are so rotten that I might as well stay home and listen to their tapes," Jessica grumbled to Elizabeth on Thursday.

"You could always take a pair of binoculars," Elizabeth said helpfully.

Jessica made a face. Even though she'd been having a little bit of trouble seeing lately, she'd never do something as silly as bringing a pair of binoculars to a concert. "My life is such a mess," she said sadly. "I lost the trip to Paris, I have a terrible seat for the concert, and I have to hear Lila go on and on about her wonderful box seat. The only thing I have to look forward to is the consolation prize Ms. Harris is sending."

Elizabeth nodded. "I'm sure it's something neat."

"Jewelry, maybe," Jessica said hopefully. "Or French perfume. I just hope it comes soon."

Jessica's consolation prize came that very afternoon, special delivery.

"It's here!" Jessica shouted excitedly. She ran into the kitchen where her mother and Elizabeth were fixing dinner. She held the box up to her ear and shook it. "If it's perfume, there must be more than one bottle. It's a big package."

"Well, open it," Mrs. Wakefield said, drying her hands on a towel. "Let's see what you've got."

Jessica tore off the wrapping paper.

"What is it?" Elizabeth asked.

Jessica held up the box. "*Voyage en France*," she read out loud. " 'A complete series of French lessons on cassette.' Oh, no," she moaned. "What a letdown!"

Mrs. Wakefield smiled. "That's really a good prize, Jessica. You can get a head start on your French, and next year, you can enter the contest again."

"No way!" Jessica dropped her face into her hands. "I told Lila I was getting perfume or jewelry! This is so awful. I'm completely humiliated!"

Mrs. Wakefield put her hand on Jessica's shoulder. "Would it make you feel any better," she asked, "if I told you about something special coming up, something that's even better than a box seat at the Dynamo concert?"

Jessica was desolate. "I don't know what could be better than a box seat at the concert," she moaned.

Mrs. Wakefield smiled. "What about a front row seat?" she asked. "One for you, one for Elizabeth, one for Steven, and one for Brooke."

"Front row seats?" Jessica and Elizabeth cried.

"Remember that decorating job I mentioned a few days ago?" Mrs. Wakefield asked Jessica. "The one Brooke's father helped me get? It's for Nick England. He just bought a house for his parents."

"Nick England?" Jessica breathed incredulously.

Elizabeth was glad that she had kept her mother's secret. Jessica was so excited.

"He was so impressed with the work I've done so far," Mrs. Wakefield explained, "that he gave me complimentary tickets for four front-row seats."

"Front-row seats!" Jessica exclaimed ecstatically. "I can't believe it. And neither will Lila!"

The concert was probably the most exciting event of Jessica's entire life.

"This is terrific!" Jessica shouted to Elizabeth, as the band began to play. She gave an ecstatic sigh. "And I can't believe how cute Nick England is. He's even cuter than he is in his pictures!"

Brooke grinned and clapped her hands. "I can't believe this!" She turned around and looked toward the sky boxes. "I wonder whether Lila can see us on her closed circuit TV."

"Who cares about Lila?" Jessica sighed dreamily, settling back and fixing her eyes on the stage. "These front-row seats are a miracle."

But the real miracle was yet to come. Halfway through the concert, Nick England leaned over the edge of the stage.

"Which of you is Jessica?" he asked with a grin.

Jessica's heart was beating as loud as Dynamo's drums. "I am," she called.

"How about a dance?" Nick asked, pulling her up on the stage. Jessica was so thrilled to be close to Nick that she forgot to be scared by the idea that the entire audience was looking at her. All she could think about was the joy of dancing with Nick England in front of thousands of people. Nothing like this had ever happened in her entire life!

The next morning, Jessica couldn't wait to get on the telephone to Lila. Now she had something really fantastic to brag about!

Lila sounded grumpy when she said hello.

"Oh, Lila," Jessica sighed happily. "I had such fun last night. Did you see me dancing with Nick England?"

"I saw," Lila said glumly.

"It was just wonderful," Jessica gushed. "To be up there on stage with all those people looking at me, and have Nick's arms around me. I just know I have to be a star when I grow up. How did I look on closed circuit TV, Lila?"

There was a pause. "I don't know." Lila sounded very grouchy. She paused. "It wasn't working last night," she admitted at last.

Jessica smothered a laugh. "It wasn't working? Oh, Lila, I'm so sorry," Jessica said as sincerely as she could. Deep down inside she was delighted, but she didn't let her voice betray her. "What a shame. Well, you had such a good seat that you probably didn't miss the TV much. What did the stage look like from the box?"

"It looked like a postage stamp," Lila said

dejectedly. "The sky box is so far away from the stage that you can't see anything without binoculars."

Now Jessica really wanted to laugh, but she didn't want to hurt Lila's feelings. "That's too bad, Lila."

"The PA system wasn't working, either," Lila added sadly. "And the concessionnaire wasn't serving the boxes. I had to walk all the way down to the lobby to get something to drink." She paused. "I really envy you, Jessica, getting those front-row seats. And getting to dance with Nick England. What luck."

"It wasn't luck," Jessica said. This time, she couldn't help bragging. "My mother got the tickets for us. She's decorating a house for Nick."

"Oh," Lila said after a minute. "Do you think that next time your mother could get a front-row seat for me, too?" she added in a small voice.

Now Jessica really *did* laugh. "Maybe," she said. "I'll ask her."

Will Jessica's good luck run out? Find out in Sweet Valley Twins #47, JESSICA'S NEW LOOK.